AUTHOR'S NOTE

When I first started writing The Group, there was more of Khaled in me than there is now. I had just left a job that paid very well but inspired me very little and had very few thoughts about what I was going to do next. All I knew at the time was that I didn't want to become one of those people who get into a groove of complaining about their lot but doing nothing about it. Luckily I have a very supportive wife, Mira, who told me my only option was to leave and to see what happens. There were a few dark days of doubt and fear, but looking back now, I can't even recognise the person who started this book. Despite all his faults, Khaled isn't such a bad person at all. He's just looking for a way to live life without fear.

RAVINDER CHAHAL

the group

reverb

reverb is an imprint of Osiris Press Ltd

This edition first published 2005 by

Osiris Press Ltd
PO Box 615
Oxford OX1 9AL

www.readreverb.com
www.osirispress.co.uk

A CIP catalogue record for this book is available from the British Library

ISBN 1 905315 01 5

Set in Baskerville 12/14.2pt
Title font Mutagen (www.fontmonster.org)

Printed in Britain by
Lightning Source, Milton Keynes

for Mira, Tom, Ken and my father

A young man walks past a shop and sees a chair in the window in 1961. He stops and looks at the chair and looks again and he knows that his uncle's house, where he stays with ten others, has been robbed. He is shocked and unsure what to do.

The chair is exactly the same as the one in his uncle's house, but he has only been staying there for three days so he has to make certain. He waits outside the shop, where it is cold and grey and the people walk on by, until he finally decides to be bold and enter, for his uncle's sake.

Inside the shop he is nervous and unsteady, keeping his head bowed and his eyes to the floor. When no-one challenges him, he looks again closely at the chair. It is his uncle's for sure, but the shiny material, which is the same as the colour of dung, is cleaner and brighter than how he remembers.

As he turns to leave he sees his uncle's lamp. And one just like it in a different colour. And at a low table, further inside the shop, he sees the plate that he ate off that morning and the cup into which he served his uncle tea, long before the anaemic sun had appeared at his small dirty window.

He is confused enough to forget his fear. He walks to the back of the shop and picks up the cup. And sees more cups and plates all identical but much greater in number than the ones in his uncle's house.

'How can it be?' He thinks. Everything in his uncle's house is here all around him and more besides.

As he looks at one cup after the next, distracted by the

perfect way they all look exactly the same even in their variations of colour and style, he does not notice the square-faced man who has approached him from behind.

'Can I... help you... sir?' asks the man with a sour tone to his voice.

The young man turns about abruptly, startled by the foreign voice, dropping the cup that is not his uncle's so that it smashes on the floor, never to be part of a perfect set again. The young man is appalled and does the only thing he can. He runs to the door and flees the scene with fear and panic in his heart, although he will laugh about what has happened for the next forty years.

This same man will also one day tell of all the jobs he once had; more than he can remember, all of them hard and dirty, but the worst he will say, is when he worked nights in a crisp factory in Leicester. The smell was stronger than the stench of a slaughterhouse or an open sewer, and the heat brutal, made worse by the sharp cold air that he knew was waiting for him outside.

He was young and strong when he had this job, but even so he was sacked after less than three weeks. He kept falling asleep on his feet, and whenever he was awoken by an angry compatriot on the night-shift, it would take him several minutes to realise that he was no longer in the grip of a nightmare.

And then there is one final story this man will often tell. Again it was the sixties, he's not sure of the year. He remembers the marvel of the first TV he ever saw: black and white, fuzzy and heavily encased in wood. A friend of his uncle's, proud as punch, asks him to turn it over to see what is on the other side. The young man stands up and approaches the set, heavy in it's cabinet. He looks at the front and the back and the sides, and seeing nothing, tries to lift the box to see what is painted on the bottom.

The man is my father and these are his stories, the only ones he tells of coming to this country, where he was a Punjabi fish out of water for so many years.

I've always valued old things; second-hand clothes, scratched-up records, fob-watches, pen-knives, medals and coins. Old things wrapped in cloth and taken down from the attic, each with a story to tell. Old dusty things that speak silently to us about the past, telling us exactly where we're from and how long we've been established in the place that we are now in.

There were never any treasures in my attic. There were no voices from the past. There were no dead men's clothes. Or any evidence of the lives that were lived that led to me. It was as if my family history started less than fifty years ago, when my grandfather came to England on a boat and eventually chose my father for his daughter as a good son-in-law.

But despite the lack of physical objects to tell us who we are, we had, for a while at least, a togetherness that shielded us from the outside, keeping us separate and apart and this reinforced the idea that we were different, although it would reveal little else. But long before our food, or our music or our industry, were celebrated as they sometimes are today, being together was all we had.

We would not be together for very long though. In a

world where the children forgot their mother tongue and spoke in a different way to the unsteady accents of their fathers, suspicion and rifts would easily grow. And the fathers, who not only came from a different place, but also from a different time, soon began to believe their children despised them and their ways.

They were brought up to obey and honour their parents, without question and without any ideas of the entitlement of self.

Perhaps the only reason they left their homes and lied about their ages to secure passage on cold ships and planes was simply because their own fathers had wished it. They were here to work, make money and send it back home and they did it all for the good of the group.

So they could not easily accept or forgive the child that would not honour or obey them in return. And perhaps they believed in their hearts that their children wanted nothing of the old world that they had had to leave behind, but had never forgotten and longed instead for the acceptance of the new. Perhaps they believed that their children wished them invisible. And silent. To make their passage and acceptance into this cold and colourless new world easier.

So in the absence of heirlooms, or togetherness, they would tell no stories either. Because they feared their children, as they feared their new world. They dreamt and eulogised a place that never had existed, and talked of respect. Without ever giving their children a chance in this world or the past.

The only link with my past was broken in exactly this way. My father lives, but we know nothing of each other.

He tells me nothing of his world and asks nothing of mine. I am alone to make my own way in the same way that he did forty years ago. But we cannot even share that bond, because his was a world of hard labour and racism and saving every penny, while I move among those whose problems are petty and whose hands are always clean.

I cannot look him in the eye and tell him of any struggle. And he won't counsel me because he fears my rejection, thinking that I have more in common with the world that he struggled against.

And now that I'm the only thing he has, he has passed on to me the one true gift he has to give, a skewed tradition that I will easily keep on: a feeling of belonging to no one place. And perhaps no one thing. Leaving me free to drift, restless and without roots.

1: WORK IT TO THE BONE

Over the last two years, Irish boy-band Cruzin has chalked up a record 12 straight number one records. This phenomenal success is due to the band's hugely loyal pre-teen fan base. While the boys' squeaky clean image and undoubted musical talents have helped build this level of schoolyard popularity, they also have a secret weapon.

PMC, Cruzin's record company, is notorious for its use of sophisticated marketing techniques. With Cruzin, it teamed up with internet marketing consultancy Torrid Media to build a powerful online tool to promote singles sales to the core under-13 pop market.

The Cruzin database contains over 250,000 email addresses and mobile phone numbers for text alerts, of which 69% belong to pre-teen girls aged between 8 and 11 – the crucial pop-single buying and mp3 downloading demographic.

These contacts have been harvested through a ruthless blitzkrieg campaign of marketing and promotions.

Blitzkrieg?

These 250,000 registered fans represent an enviable source of market intelligence, which means PMC is able to target promotions with smart-bomb accuracy.

In return the tagged and numbered fans receive access to 'exclusive' materials, including sneak previews of videos, new releases, ring-tones and even interactive webcasts, where they get to chat to their pop idols online.

Tagged and numbered? C'mon now. Don't push it.

Torrid's founder, CEO and Chief Strategic Tinkerer, Philip Mould, says: 'Its an exceptionally effective system, harnessing powerful Internet-based and mobile technologies to maximise the marketing potential that these kids represent. The result speaks for itself.'

There, there. That's more like it. Powerful, thrusting, meaty platitudes that fill up the mouth.

'The Torrid system works on a basis of incentive and rewards. Every time a fan buys a single, they receive a unique access code, which earns them special Cruzin Credits. The more credits they accrue the more special features they are able to access on the band's website.'

While this is a powerful tool in itself, there is a further element to this ingenious solution that can virtually ensure the band a number one hit with each release.

As part of the marketing hype prior to a new single, registered fans are primed with an e-flyer or text alert from the band which contains a time-limited offer, usually a competition to meet the band, or back-stage passes to a show. To enter they must buy the new single on a specific day of the week so it will register highest in the midweek charts.

The most dedicated fans can even earn special multiplier Cruzin Credits by buying the single in several different formats on the day of release, to fast-track them up the Cruzin Credit fan ladder.

Christ, what a smug little scheme. I don't quite know how I can go on writing this stuff.

Is it just me? Has no one else noticed? Is this kind of thing really ok with everyone else? I honestly don't know, I just can't tell the difference any more.

Where I once would have been so sure and secure in my opinions, I'm now lost and seem unable to discriminate between what is praiseworthy and that which is truly depressing.

Maybe I'm not the only one. Rather than wrinkle our noses in distaste at this sour little scheme, most of us will let it slip right by without question or comment.

Worse still, there are those who'll get on board. They'll embrace the concept and applaud its brutal simplicity, while daydreaming about the numbers involved. As if being able to understand the USP, replaces the need to know the difference between right and wrong.

But come on, what are we really talking about here? Using the internet to tempt nine-year-old girls. Tapping them up to spend, spend, spend. Hairless bodies and gleaming white teeth as bait for the hook. What a beautiful way to make your money.

See, there you go again. Thinking not writing. Wasting time. If I lose momentum, this piece will sink into the afternoon and creep into next week. I need to stop stalling and fulfil my obligations.

But it's already too late. What I need now is a diversion. Some piece of mischief to distract myself and force me over the finish line.

Sometimes I might try a deliberate overdose of business power-gibberish. Jargonate, confuse and go technical. Slip it into the mouth of some poor innocent client CEO. Chief. Executive. Officer.

Who would ever think to question a six-figure salary man, when he talks of the need to 'upskill the knowledge asset and seamlessly integrate the key resource that is our team' or become 'customer-centric in the 24-hour availability age for absolute peak market penetration'.

Or I might conjure up a statistic. '69% of pre-teen girls aged between 8 and 11 – the crucial pop-single buying demographic.' Sometimes the numbers can feel so right they really ought to be true. And it's a queerly satisfying thrill when someone repeats your phantom numbers back to you two or three weeks later, once your little bird of a lie has finally taken wing.

So what about the Torrid Cruzin honey trap? Using the internet to reel in little children, where can I go with that?

Philip Mould believes the band's success is due to its special relationship with its fans: 'PMC has unrestricted access to these children. Our system provides a direct channel into their bedrooms. We talk to them in a language they understand, tapping into their wants and desires to connect in a way that their parents can only dream of.'

'And these children are not passive. They don't just sit there and take it as we pump more into them. They are more than willing to take part. So while their parents are downstairs watching News at Ten, having put their kids to bed, Cruzin is upstairs in their children's bedrooms, giving them exactly what they want.'

A little heavy-handed perhaps, but I'm not going to rewrite it. I hate having to correct my work – then again, I rarely have to.

Of course, it has to get past the account handler and approved by the client, but I get the feeling that they must skim more than they actually read.

As long as the client's name and picture appears high up enough and often enough, and the language is suitably ponderous, everyone seems to go home happy. And as for the journalists and the editors whose job it is to question, check facts and cut through the spin, the only thing I need to remind myself is that there is a huge ravenous beast out there that depends on an endless stream of pictures and copy, day after day, to sustain it.

So I won't rewrite it. All I need is a headline. Something sufficiently tacky and obvious: *Torrid Media and Cruzin – a chart-topping duo*. They'll definitely go for that.

It may sound awful but I've even lost the thrill of trying

15

to get away with deliberately bad writing. Especially once I finally realised that the more awful I would try to be, the more praise I would actually receive.

Suffice to say I am now much sought after as a skilled and well-respected technician in my field.

Still, even I have a little pride that I occasionally indulge, that may yet mess the ointment.

Let me think: *How PMC Music bought boy-band Cruzin a run of Torrid number ones.*

A quick sugar rush of rebellion. Who knows? If nothing else it may catch the eye of a jaded news editor. And that's what it's all about, making your release stand out from the other 49 he receives that day.

Spell-check and send? Fuck it. It's done. And it's still only 4.30 in the afternoon. Spell-check and send.

2: EASY LISTENING

I heard somebody on the radio this morning talking about Generation X. And Y and Z. I almost immediately turned him off. I find our incessant need to label, quantify and analyse our lives or, worse still, our lifestyles, a vapid form of entertainment.

But something he said struck a chord so I listened on. Just a single phrase. 'They are successful stakeholders in an economy that they simply don't believe in.'

It's a thought that been ringing through my head, blocking my attempts to go quietly through the day.

I've been left feeling reckless and anxious at the same time. As if I might do something rash but I'm not sure what it may be. Maybe it's nothing to do with the radio programme.

Actually his voice of professional opinion lost me when he went on to say that, unlike generations of the past such as the fabled 60s, we did not drop-out. According to him we 'co-opted protest, and safely marketed rebellion as a cool, commercial product'.

Which sounds like bullshit to me. Just another version of the good old days.

Still I'm not sure why I'm feeling this way. There may even be something quite seriously wrong with me.

In fact, this is quite a common thought for me. That I'm being betrayed by my own body at the most basic micro-cellular level. Rogue chemical reactions, defective genes, a misfiring neuron or receptor. Weapons of micro-destruction.

The human body, such a marvellous and complex machine to maintain. So much to go wrong. Such responsibility. And then there's me who can barely change a light bulb let alone manage and maintain such a sophisticated piece of kit.

And even assuming that all is well for now and I've managed to postpone the inevitable, there's no getting away from that fact that I'm just not feeling right.

I never really do. I have my own peculiar problem. A very special syndrome.

You see I have this thing about lying. A compulsion perhaps, or even a disorder.

Maybe it's something I ate. I may well be infected by some diseased beef carcass. Or a chemical-pink salmon that once thrashed snout to tail, mass-farmed in a murky, brown water.

But I'm vegetarian so it can't be that.

Still there must be something that absolves me. A trite little label that I'm yet to find.

All I know is that telling lies is so easy.

You know what? It's almost too easy. People will believe almost anything you tell them. Do almost anything you ask.

Think about it.

Too much choice. Too much information. And it never pays to show you're a little confused. Lost, bewildered.

Not when everyone seems so sure of themselves. Sure of their opinions, professional or otherwise. Their brands. Their leanings. The tribe they represent. Confident. Smug. Self-possessed. Expressing themselves creatively through every decision they make, every item they consume, every life-experience they broadcast.

But take your time. Look a little closer. Notice the bitten nails. The red rimmed eyes. The papery skin. Turn down the noise, the chat, the trivia and the gossip. Filter out the mania. Hear what people are really saying, if anything at all.

See how they drink. Take drugs. Couple. Create dramas and distractions to call their own. And you'll appreciate the scale of the situation. The stress, the sticky tension, the cloying pressure and the ever present strain.

This isn't what any of us thought our lives were going to be. We're supposed to be special, remember. We're supposed to be fulfilled and make our mark. Leave something behind to remembered by.

Our lives are meant to be great journeys of discovery, where we will find ourselves. And love. Experience great sex. Multiple partners. Experiment. Fidelity. Forever.

The brochure says we will stay youthful. But grow. And change and develop.

And then there is money. We must make it. Lots and lots of it. But it mustn't define us. It mustn't be a goal in itself. Instead we must do something important. Make a difference. And we must love our work. And our second or third career.

We need to create. Be creative. And social. And interesting. But not the same. We must each be individuals. Perfect snowflakes each and everyone.

So who can face the thought that they haven't managed to fit all that in? That they don't quite measure up?

When all around us we're surrounded by people who scream out life is great, life is great? Allah. Akhbar.

So we condition ourselves to believe. And keep on believing. Suckling up to any little lie that soothes and distracts us.

Or helps us cope with the fact we aren't really coping, and that we are unsure. Self-conscious. Awkward. Angry. Helpless.

So let's huddle together for warmth. Take refuge in the group and all its kind-hearted deceptions. Safe. Regimented. Sedated with rules and conventions. Triggers. Responses and rewards.

Let us lose ourselves among the many and help us forget the pain of who we are and, I promise you, we'll all believe any warm and merciful lie.

3: DOCK OF THE BAY

Looking around the office I can see that everyone else is either in meetings, on the telephone or preparing press lists. I'll keep my head down until after five so no one can ask me to start on anything else.

I get up from my desk and navigate round my colleagues. Our open-plan office is an unnatural rat's nest of workstations, desks, chairs, screen dividers and people all squeezed in together, each of them jealously guarding their personal three feet of space. Looking at it and listening to it makes me dizzy and tense.

I spend twenty minutes locked in a cubicle in the men's toilets just staring at the tiled floor between my knees. Counting the cracks. Marking out time.

Even in here I cannot truly relax, it's too cold and every noise is amplified, harsh and metallic, but at least I can sit with a solid wall behind me rather than the creeping feeling of eyes on my back.

It's not that anyone will be looking at me, they're all plugged into their own little pods, getting on with what they need to do, but it's an unsettling feeling that I can't shake, not knowing what's going on behind my back.

And then there's the constant noise of the other people with their jarring phone-calls and their banal, inane chatter. It's almost unbearable. I find it impossible to filter out. The others are immune. They seem so comfortable in their skins, and unaware of their shared surroundings. Or their impact upon it.

They just get on with it and have no idea what they're doing to me, but I swear I can physically feel the irritation and taut annoyance rising in my bones and creeping through my joints and muscles.

People say 'relax' like it's an easy thing, but for me it's a slow torture that I have to endure every night in order to finally sleep.

Visualisation helps. I fantasise about just walking out of the building for a few hours and returning to find that, rather than missing me, or wondering where I've been, no one in the office knows me at all.

I return to my desk. Check my emails. There is an endless chain of jokes that aren't funny and smut that gets more extreme and less arousing by the day.

Delete. Delete. Delete.

An email from Jun, my flatmate: he wants to know if we are going out this Saturday and if I have spoken to someone about getting something. I haven't and don't reply.

Another one from Tom, a senior account manager in my team. A diligent reminder to us that we are all expected to go out for a drink tonight to welcome the new work experience boy. Again I don't reply.

And a new email, just received, from Quentin, partner and overall head of team.

Which is a bit of a shock. Not the email so much as the fact he's still in the office on a Friday afternoon. Looking up, I can just see him from my desk, in his little cupboard office, blinds down, door closed.

On Fridays, if he's not 'working from home', he usually rings in from an afternoon meeting to say that it is running on and that he 'might not make it back to the office'.

Maybe he's sticking around because we're having drinks for the new boy, a chance to survey his little fiefdom and drone on about how much fun we are to work with.

His email says that he has just received the Torrid Media piece and that he wants to have a word with me on Monday morning.

When I first started as a writer, on a trade newspaper, I would try to craft every sentence and carve out every word, with the naïve thought that I would be leaving them behind to stand the test of time. When I started as a copywriter I thought it was my duty to understand every client's business so as to represent them fairly and accurately.

Now I'm little more than a machine. I switch on and off. And I have almost perfect lack of recall. Even though I only finished the piece thirty minutes ago, I have absolutely no idea what I wrote.

I reply to Quentin asking him what time we'll meet and again I'm surprised to see an almost immediate reply. He says that he'll see me first thing on Monday before the day really starts.

For 'first thing' read 10.30 at the earliest but even so he's a bit keen.

Shit, what did I write in that piece?

4: GLASSHOUSES, THROWING STONES

Timing is a beautiful thing. At this moment, The Ship is like a slave ship, it's so overcrowded with grey, navy-blue and pinstriped bodies sweating into their suits.

None of us has a seat and Tom has been standing hopelessly forlorn at the bar, clutching his company Amex from the moment we arrived.

In an hour the place will be desolate and empty, with listless bar staff emptying ash-trays and picking up glasses from deserted tables. But by then we'll be gone too, and in the meantime we'll have to stand far too close to each other.

White and gold cigarette boxes appear as if by magic. My perennial ten-pack signifies that I'm not really a smoker, but lighting up gives us all an opportunity to step back before we have to engage.

We are huddled in a tight group near the back of the bar, waiting for Tom to return with the drinks. The team: Rhys, Gemma, Quentin, Ben, the new boy and myself. I keep a close eye on Quentin but he's giving nothing away.

Instead he is asking Gemma what she is doing at the weekend, both of them hyper-aware that they are conducting a conversation in front of an audience.

The challenge of their own little chat-show. The unspoken pressure to project personality and amuse.

Listening in on Gemma is an education in tight-rope walking. Until recently an uncomplicated small-town girl, she is now in a constant state of self-renewal. Like a lizard shedding its skin.

After graduation she flew the nest and took her first

faltering steps towards taking on the big city life: career, clothes, love-life and all.

Her plain face is now painted and framed by a highlighted salon cut, her midriff newly toned and emaciated after an unmitigated assault of sit-ups and salads, and her dumpy legs are elongated and squeezed into a set of cruel City-girl bondage boots.

Six or seven weeks ago her long-term university boyfriend fell victim to her grand makeover. We all watched and listened to the tense phone calls and observed how, as the drama unfolded, Gemma became welcomed further into the sorority of unattached workplace girls who meet for lunch or get together at the weekends. If they're not dating, that is.

As other avenues of opportunity and advancement have opened up, her old life including boyfriend have been quickly forgotten. Now thin, single and available, her transformation is nearly complete. She seems invigorated, more assertive and sure of herself, as if her life now has some higher meaning.

All that remains of old self is her round and slightly squashy backside, like a despised vestigial reminder of what she's left behind.

'We're going to School's Out,' she says to Quentin, trying to mask her discomfort by taking on the patronising demeanour a teen will take with an embarrassing parent or 'trendy' uncle.

'Yeah it should be really good. We haven't been before, but we thought we'd check it out. Should be a laugh. My new housemates are gonna come. So it'll be a bottle of wine and getting ready at ours first and then out on the town.'

Gemma always appears to talk in the plural and I have noticed that she collects people. At work, her desk is decorated with pictures of her mates. Many of these have changed recently. Whenever she comes back from holidays, the 'piccies' are always passed around.

And apart from the odd one of her in a bikini, the only thing I have noticed is that all of her pictures always feature a crowd of faces. They are always a 'good bunch' or a 'right laugh', but no one person ever seems to stand out as the focal point. All I ever see is blur of grinning faces that I find hard to tell apart, be they male or female.

Quentin asks a question with wet-lipped intent: 'School's Out? Isn't that where everyone dresses up in school uniform and gets off with each other? I read about it in the Sunday supplement. Are you gonna be dressing up?'

I can see that Gemma is instantly wary of the question and acutely aware of the judgemental ears that are listening in. She knows that she is unfairly seen as rather a lightweight in the office but she is taking sadly predictable steps to counter this by developing a blinkered aggressive streak to match her carefully calculated PR-girl uniform. Which is a shame. She used to be quite nice.

So her instincts are now fine-tuned to pick up the faintest tremor of perceived criticism within the group. She's not having that, not from Quentin. Not from anyone.

'Yeah they do play all these old records from the eighties, so we might do the eighties dress-up, but it's a retro thing. You're right there has been a lot of press about it but I don't think everyone really gets it. D'you know what I mean? And anyway it's a girl's night out so the rule is no boys. Just a bit of laugh with the girlies'.'

I wonder who'll be first to break ranks, and how successful each of the girls will be. Pecking orders will be established as well as new rifts and resentments.

I must be smirking because Gemma notices that I have been listening in. She may be predictable but she intuitively knows how to turn defence into attack. If you want to get ahead you have to leapfrog others. If you feel yourself being put into a box, be quick to pass judgement or stereotype others. Especially if it is in front of the boss.

'You know what though it is getting pretty big now. Maybe we could all go to it. Like a team night out. Better than hanging out in here every Friday. We could get dressed up and have a boogie. Then again, I'm not sure about Khaled though, it might not be cool enough for him.'

Oh I do detest her now. I know I shouldn't really care but I'm sputtering at the fact that I have no withering put-down ready to spit back in her face.

Tom returns with the drinks and cuts me off before I can come up with anything approaching a suitable reply. So instead, I turn to face him and give her my back.

'Let's rescue the new boy,' he says.

Over the past few days Ben, our new work experience guy, has quickly established himself as an enthusiastic, earnest and optimistic young man. He has shown himself to be willing, helpful and polite and almost naively nice but looking at him now, I can see that even he is trying to edge away from Rhys, who has him trapped in conversation.

Rhys, the hair-gelled Welsh Wizard. The little big man. Our in-house waste of space. Within minutes of meeting him, people are instantly reduced to contacts and stored away in his executive handheld organiser.

Anyone within five yards is given the same bittersweet thumbnail of his life. In his mind, he is a player and is going places but his sense of injustice, the fact that he feels sorely wronged, is what really comes flooding through.

At first you may feel empathy, a kindred soul. A fellow traveller. Us against them. A classic mistake, because then it starts. The name-dropping. Sexy Welsh and Social? The tales of his past high-flying career before his calculated move into PR. The talk of how he shrewdly bought into London property at just the right time, quickly followed by the inevitable question – 'Do you rent or have you bought yourself?'

Then the desperate hunger to find out how much you earn and the realisation that he is on a pitiful salary. You don't have to guess, he actually tells you in the hope that you will reciprocate.

And finally the long bitter attack on all those worthless people around him, who are all useless at their jobs. The ones who make him look bad because they haven't got a clue. The ones that dump all the shitty work on him and then take all the credit. Those that should listen to someone with real world experience but hide behind the fact that they are managers. Especially the ones that are the same age, or God forbid, even younger than him.

All he wants to do is play with the big boys, gain their respect and he'll clamber all over you in his rush to get to them. Or crawl in the mud. Or bend over. Whatever it takes. Which everyone knows. He's so eager to please, but nothing ever seems to work. They don't want him yapping at their heels. No one does.

Of course he has irons in the fire. He'll be leaving soon. Onwards and upwards. Contacts. Powerful people. Stored and collected in his little magic box.

Which is why people are constantly moving away from tubby little Rhys. He has his own little no-fly zone into which only those that are hopelessly off-course ever venture and only the truly tragic remain.

Tom's right, it's time to rescue the new boy.

Rhys is quickly left standing on the periphery of the group peering in over our shoulders. He starts to gulp down his pint and suck up an evil smelling slim cigar as we throw Ben a lifeline.

'So how do you find working at Silverback so far?' asks Tom.

'Yeah it's been really good, a really nice bunch of people. Takes a bit of getting used to though. It's all a bit different from uni, especially getting up so early every day and having to wear a suit,' he says with a smile. 'Hopefully I'll get the hang of it soon and I'll be able to make myself useful and stop bothering you lot with stupid questions.'

Tom and I both know that Ben is no student slacker. Reading his CV when he applied for work experience gave me a hot queasy feeling. He gets involved. Does extra-curricular activities, plays sport, gets elected to student bodies. At 21, he gives the impression that he's already working towards something and seems to have a sense of where he is going. In less than a week he has become a trusted, valuable part of the team. His upbeat attitude is infectious, and he is disarmingly modest.

And the strangest thing is, that despite all of this, I can't bring myself to dislike him.

Quentin comes over, looking at his watch. 'Ben I'm going to leave you with this lot. Take care they don't get you in any trouble tonight.' Half a drink and he's off, dutifully hurrying back to Surrey to his growing brood of children, and his big comfortable wife who smells of powdered milk.

He turns to me before bustling towards the door. 'Remember Khaled, first thing on Monday morning.'

'Yes right Quentin. I'll be there nice and early, No worries.' But he's already on his way.

'What's happening on Monday,' asks Rhys, ferreting in closer.

'Sorry mate, can't tell you. New project, senior management and essential staff only. I had to sign an NDA.'

Tom, gives me a 'why do you bother?' face. He instantly knows I'm winding Rhys up and can't really see the point. I sometimes forget he's management. But I've got the sniff now.

'Maybe I can help,' says Rhys. 'You can tell us something can't you?'

'Sorry mate I don't know much myself. All I know is that the partners have asked me to keep quiet. You know what they're like. And anyway I'll probably only be doing a bit of copywriting.'

I can see Gemma bright-eyed and interested now. It's

too tempting to resist. 'Listen, it's really not that interesting. All I can say is that we might be doing something with a new client that might involve a big celebrity fashion magazine, and there's a chance that we'll need a venue for an event that they think is, you know, cool enough. So you know what they're like, they've asked me to help out.'

'Who's working on it?' she asks. While Rhys will try the direct approach, she'll be straight onto the network of assistants and secretaries to find out what she can.

'Sorry I don't know and even if I did, I can't say.'

'Fucking typical isn't it?' says Rhys, 'They're always going on about open door policy and sharing expertise. But whenever anything good comes along, it's all secrets and every man for himself.'

'What do you know about it then, Tom?' he demands.

'I've heard nothing,' says Tom glaring at me.

'Saying nothing, more like,' mutters Rhys, hurt but belligerent.

'Honest mate I don't know what Khaled's talking about. Anyway, remember we're not supposed to be talking about work, it's Friday night and we are meant to be having a nice little drink so Ben can get to know us. We don't want to give him the wrong impression now do we?'

'So where are we going?' I ask.

'I thought you knew all the best places Khaled,' says Gemma.

'Only some of them Gemma. Why don't you make a suggestion? You must know a fun place where we can all have night out as a team.'

'No I can't tonight. I'm meeting someone,' she replies glancing deliberately at her watch. 'Actually I'd better be off, I don't want to keep him waiting. Well not too long.'

I make a point of not asking where she's going or who she is meeting and smile sweetly as she turns and also heads for the exit.

As soon as she is out of earshot, Rhys pipes up. 'Right then, lads' night out is it then, boys?'

5: WEST END BOYS

Another night in Soho and I'm waiting for something to happen. One place after the next. Always trying to remember the name of the doorman, the manager or the girl behind the clipboard. Scavengers trying to pick up scraps for free. Scrabbling with our phones, making last minute rendezvous. Punctuating the night by trying to work out who's holding all the chemicals.

I don't know how I got like this. I remember when I was younger, before I came to London, my thinking seemed very different.

The small city where I grew up had little to offer. There were no guest lists, no VIP. But we always felt an excitement about the things we did that we could call our own. Music we felt that no one else knew about. Clothes that we put together ourselves. A language that excluded those on the outside.

But of course it all got co-opted, sucked into the mainstream. Just like most of the kids that I shared those times with. Just like me. Music doesn't matter anymore, the clothes I wear are stylish, expensive and they keep step with all the right magazines, but they are chosen by somebody else, probably far older and nastier than me.

Being with Ben has filled me with a manic desperation to impress. I want him to know how hip and urbane I am. Force-feed him.

I drag him from one place to the next. Each one louder, faster and more soulless than the last.

I'm aware of what I'm doing. I know it's a mistake. And I'll regret perpetuating this image of myself. But I can't slow down now. Not once the ride has begun. There'll be no getting off until the sky starts to change colour and we stumble out into the first light like newborns.

Rhys has tumbled off early, but Tom is still with us on the faint promise of adulterated powders and more brightly coloured drinks. With brightly coloured people. All glitter and paste. Shouting maniacally, jostling, spitting in each other's faces.

I call acquaintances. We meet. Notes are fumbled. A walk on the wild side for all concerned. I take on the role of the tour-guide. Demeaning myself. Performing like a stage-monkey.

Ben asks questions. Wants to know more about me. He looks even younger now his face is red and flushed with alcohol. And I still can't stop. I introduce him to shadow people. Leering, knowing, fellow freaks on show.

They make me nervous. Unsure. My heart beats faster. Skin glows with sweat. Grime under my nails. Grit and dirt all around. Walls and surfaces finger damp, sticky.

Ben is wide-eyed. I tell him stories, I tell him lies.

It's all just glitter and paste anyway. Smoke and mirrors. And I always put on a show.

6: BELLY-BUTTON

In his interview, Ben told Tom and Quentin that he will be managing director of his own company before he's 35. And that he intends to use everything he learns and experiences in the meantime to bring about his goal.

I am told he said this with great calm, no irony, no embarrassment, no posturing or showing off. Just matter of fact. Tom says that it was quite a thing to see.

And something about that has been getting under my skin, agitating me. I feel a certain unwarranted resentment towards him. I want to blame him for something, but I'm not sure what. My instinctive reaction is to turn on him or undermine him in some way, but in truth I'm actually quite frightened by him.

Looking back, I cringe with guilty loathing at the memory of the places I took him to and the way I so crassly tried to dazzle and impress. I am nothing but a brittle fake.

But I'll get over it. I routinely play the fool and have learnt to live with it.

No, it's not that that fuels my resentment.

And it's not his ambition, or even the fact he stated it openly for all to hear. There are plenty of people who possess the kind of drive I know nothing about, just as there are those that are full of bluster and simply repeat what they think they ought to be saying. I've come across them before and it's never bothered me like this.

It's not even that he's young and hopeful. I usually equate that with stupidity, whether it's fair or not.

The thing that gets to me is the fact that he can look

into his own future with some certainty and make choices for himself.

I'm nearly 35, the age at which his dreams are scheduled to come true, but the idea of having to define myself by what I want out of life is as terrifying as it is bewildering.

There's simply no substance to back up my bluff, so I can never show my hand in the way Ben has.

All I have are worries: what if I make the wrong choice? What makes one choice better than another? What if I say I'm going to do something and don't make it?

I'm lost at sea. I simply don't know how to play the game, because somewhere I fear there's a set of rules that have been kept secret from me.

So instead of making choices or taking decisions like Ben, I've just drifted, and become very good at putting people down.

I know what I don't want and can quite easily define myself by what I reject but just recently I've started to realise that this leaves me with very little that I can call my own.

Career-wise, I know that I never wanted to be a square accountant or lawyer. Or work in the City or be a doctor. Especially not as an Indian. I can't abide the thought of fitting into someone's stereotype. I still don't want anyone to think they know something about me or that they can shoehorn me into some two-line description.

Sure it was what my parents wanted. They were poor and uneducated when they came to this country, but not stupid. Far from it in fact.

My mother especially, denied the chance to study by an early arranged marriage, always revered education and subsequent position in society above all else. She was brilliant at calendar sums, and long division and tried to get me to be the same. Drumming it into me after school, when all I wanted to do was watch Monkey or The Six Million Dollar Man. She honestly thought that if you work hard and apply yourself, you will get your rewards.

Respect in the family, status in the community, a good education, good job, children who respect their parents, children who do as their parents say, children you can be proud of.

That's all I got as I was growing up. And for a while I showed real potential, passing exams to get into private school. But no scholarship. Making my dad work seven days a week to pay for it. Five days on an assembly line, then Saturday and Sunday delivering spices and rice and vegetables to Indian grocery shops that never sleep. All to pay for my mother's ambition.

She worked too, doing fine embroidery, piece-work in a factory, working on military insignia, epaulets and badges that signified power and rank. On the outside looking in, straining her eyes and ruining her soft loving hands.

And I was obliged to feel the pressing weight of sacrifice and duty.

I saw how my mother always seemed to have a feeling of shame, the inferiority that comes from being displaced. An immigrant. One part of her in the past, and the remainder always invested into a future nirvana, leaving nothing for the now.

And then came her cousins, the ones over whom she had age and authority at home. They arrived and overtook her.

Universities. Degrees. Doctors. Lawyers. Success stories. They never called her worker-girl, but she heard it, anyway.

My father worked hard, but he was never able to take a risk. He had no brothers or cousins in England to go into business with. Instead he sent money home.

So we stood still and she switched all her ambition to me. Pushing me, always pushing me. To do well in my exams, to get to a private school. To go to university. To get into Oxford. Something she can be proud of. Something she can boast about to aunties and uncles. I never once had to think for myself.

So I arrived at Oxford, always with the terrifying shadow of arranged marriage waiting at the end of it, grinding ever closer an inch at a time. Something I never wanted, something that set me apart from all the other kids, something that made me fear that I would lose my family, break their hearts when I would finally have to betray their plans for me by saying no.

I became good at keeping my thoughts from her at an early age. Good at telling little white lies to her and the rest of my family, so as not to shame them or hurt them in any way. Good at leading a double life and playing a part, and keeping my secrets from the bright new friends I made at college.

College. A stay of execution. Drugs, partying, music. Too cool for school. Too cool to make any choices. Too cool to apply myself. Let off the leash, free and unable to think about the future. Limbo. Outside. Looking nowhere.

And then she died. Cancer. In my second year. Setting me free from all the expectations and the dread. Setting me adrift.

7: THE WAR. ON DRUGS

Jun and I have been friends since school. His father came over from Japan as a motor industry executive. He settled with his dainty wife in a small, one-storey house in a pretty village just outside of town. A small neat house. Everything in its place. Picture-perfect like a fairy-tale

He had two children in this house. Jun, and his older brother Go.

Go fulfilled all his father's expectations. He was an awkward boy, slightly overweight, but a dutiful son. And he achieved all the things that he was meant to do.

Jun always seemed more blessed. From an early age, the light shone on him and around him; he was a carefree, sociable and beautiful boy. Throughout our teens, everyone instantly took a liking to sweet-natured Jun, who had a God-given talent for giving people his warmth and his full attention, making them feel good and special.

But he liked video games and skateboarding and then art and music, much more than school. He simply could not match the achievements of his brother or the standards set by his father.

No matter how hard he tried, he couldn't do well. He got it into his head that he wasn't any good. Not at school, nor at art college. And it affected him. Knocked his confidence. Made him put things off. Look for distractions. Avoid dealing with things. Avoid taking charge of himself.

And when his disapproving father finally retired, he returned to Japan. Sold his house. Packed up his belongings and left for the other side of the world. Taking his wife. Go soon followed. The perfect family together. Leaving Jun to his friends.

We came down to London together and have stuck together even though we used to fall out month after month when we moved into our first sweaty sock of a flat.

We have a bigger, cleaner place now and have reached an understanding. We're now used to each other's ways and try to avoid the tough subjects. I'm less of a bully now too, which helps us get along and he is a bit more forthcoming and less passive, which always used to frustrate me. And the weekends bind us together.

Tonight we are in a dark and sticky club. The music is loud and disposable. Black women with powerful voices singing sweet gospel melodies to blissed out clubbers. And I can see Jun carefully breaking off half a powdery, bitter-tasting pill between his teeth. His eyes are darting around to make sure no-one can see, but I've caught him in the act so he furtively passes me the other half.

'What's the matter with you?'

'Nothing I'm fine.'

'No really are you alright mate, you've been really quiet all night.'

'No really I'm fine.'

'You sure mate? I've still another half. Do you want it?

They're really good.'

'No I'm alright mate, you should take it yourself.'

'What you don't want it?'

'No I'm fine.'

'Are you sure you're alright?'

And so on and so on and so on.

The thing about Jun nowadays is that most of the time he is very unimposing and can be almost annoyingly shy and quiet, but when he's taken a pill he suddenly has a lot to say.

He came to ecstasy late on but truly loves taking pills like no one else I know. With most people, ecstasy is about dancing or sex, and becomes a routine but necessary element of a night out, popped without second thought or any real appreciation. With Jun it's quite different. The pill he takes cures him. It makes him ten feet tall. It clears away all blockages; the nervousness, politeness and inhibitions that stop him from saying what's on his mind, or acting in whatever way he feels.

He becomes that carefree beautiful boy again, talking nonsense, with a long-forgotten smile on his face.

Which is good for him but you have to be in the mood for it, and right now I'm not.

He's right something is bothering me, making the mask slip.

And the drugs I've taken are having the absolute opposite effect, making me feel introverted and distant from all the dancers who jerk their bodies and twist their faces into awful grinding smiles.

Miserable thoughts have been clouding my head since I spoke with Ben. Just the idea of all the different paths his life could take has left me feeling bereaved. I still want to blame him for something.

Jun presses his glowing face closer to mine and starts babbling something. I make like I can't hear him over the music, and use my hand to signal that I'm off to get a drink, leaving him standing in the middle of the dance floor.

The pill I've taken is making my legs feel weak and heavy, and all of a sudden my insides feel hot. I need to sit down, but I'll get some water first.

I'm hyper-conscious of all the bodies pressed against me and have to be careful where I put my hands.

There is a girl at the bar who catches my eye. Pretty, blonde, fresh. I smile immediately, without any fear. She smiles back.

Why can't it always be this easy?

She tells me her name. I can't think of anything to say, so I carry on smiling. She tells me she is with her mates, who are out on the dancefloor. She tells me what she's taken. I'm conscious that she's leaning against me.

We get our waters and walk over to a long bench lining the wall where we find a space to sit down. It all seems so natural. Her forearm rests on my leg as she twists round to face me.

She seems really young. I ask her. She tells me nineteen and already I know I can't do it. Not with my soft body. Not with the pill inside me. Not with a nineteen-year-old.

She asks me how old I am. I say 26. I mean 34. I feel like an old freak. My palms are clammy, my jaw is working away. I can feel a slug-trail of sweat sliding its way down my spine. She has such clear blue eyes. I know nothing but fear.

I start to talk. The first thing that comes into my mind. I begin to tell her I'm out on a stag do. One lie oozes into another and I start to believe.

I tell her I'm with a big group. They are all out on the dancefloor. I tell her we are all doing little missions as part of the stag do. I say we all have to bring back a souvenir from someone we've talked to.

She leans into me and asks me what kind of thing. I say it depends how much you like me. I can feel the back of her hand resting on my thigh.

She says she'll give me her number. I say no. It has to be an object. She feels part of the lie. She plays along and asks me what I want. I tell her it's up to her to decide.

She pretends to think about it, and then, reaches under her skirt. She wriggles her legs together, bends down towards her feet and quickly hands me her panties. They are like a warm, crumpled handkerchief in my hand.

The thrill of the lie is more real than what she's just done. And I begin to forget myself.

I feel a tap on my shoulder. I turn to see Jun, smiling patiently. He's looking at my new friend, waiting for me to say something. And I realise that I can't remember her name.

I do it all the time. Whenever I'm out. Especially when I'm drunk or high. Tell lies to strangers. Convince myself. Make them believe.

I tell them, I'm scouting locations. I tell them I'm with

a bunch of people that I'm trying to ditch. I tell cab-drivers that I've been to their country, grew up with their people. I say that I'm divorced with children or that my ex has just turned up.

Sometimes I'm gay, sometimes I'm celibate, teetotal and deeply religious. I pretend to know something they don't. I tell them there are hidden cameras in the loos or that the bouncer is selling coke. I make up weird and wonderful stories of where I've been, what I'm doing and how they can help.

Sometimes I know what I'm doing, mostly I don't. Jun has caught me out a couple of times, but no one else knows. He thinks that I am on a power-trip. He thinks that I have to prove that I'm cleverer than other people. Better than other people. He has warned me that if I'm not careful I'll get my comeuppance in some major way.

He might be right.

If I were on a chat-show, on after most people have gone to work, they'd give me a reason. A neat little explanation, studio-managed to fit between the ad-breaks. I might even cry gratefully onscreen. I'd get understanding, warmth and support. There may be some tough love. Perhaps some counselling. Commitments would be made. I'd reach a turning point. A pivotal moment. Live for the viewers at home.

And I'd exit stage right, knowing exactly what to do with the rest of my life.

8: MIX AND MATCH

Monday morning and I'm still hung-over from the long weekend. Partying with Jun Saturday night into Sunday morning. The old 'all back to mine' routine to carry on thumping out the tunes and racking out the lines. Sharing a few twilight hours with strangers that I rush to make my own.

The good news is that my meeting with Quentin hasn't happened yet. It's been put back till after lunch. So nothing much to do until three, when he'll get back slightly sleepy and red in the cheeks.

I keep my head down until 10.30 or so and then make my way over to the communal area, where I make a coffee, and sit with the papers.

Tom follows me over. He looks as bad as I do. Grey skin and dry old lips, but I know that my eyes will be redder than his.

'How was your weekend?' I croak.

'Rough and messy, mate, very messy.'

We talk like this almost every Monday, about mid-morning, when the headaches have subsided and we are just about ready to face the world. And often midweek too. Comparing notes.

We all mix and match every weekend, whatever's on the go. With Tom, he's more likely to leave London for the weekend. With his crowd to camp in the fields somewhere. All very earthy.

Smoking powerful weed. Drinking tins of strong lager. Taking mushrooms. And pills. And if anyone has any coke? Some of the people he hangs around with even take speed, which I do think is dodgy.

When I met them they all seemed like such perfectly mundane people. White. Middle class. Upper middle class. Public school. All very pleasant.

They often gather in one of their parents' country homes. And en masse they behave like crusty students. But they're not. They're all in their mid to late thirties. And in the week they wear suits. They have responsible jobs that need to be explained. They have people who work for them. Careers ahead of them.

Some of them are married. A few have children. They are almost all in long-term stable relationships. They see themselves as serious people. Well-used to position and privilege, but they have not quite settled down. They let their hair down at the weekends and indulge their secret lives. Looking at some of them, you'd really never guess.

And Tom is just one of the gang.

The other thing we speak about of course is quitting Silverback to do something else. A sideways move to a more fulfilling life.

A fairly common theme. We sit and we moan. And talk about leaving. Tom has a five year plan. Get married to his girlfriend. Move out of London. Spend more time in the country. Maybe by the sea, where he can buy a boat. Have babies.

Or perhaps, travel back to South America, where he once spent a gap year teaching English in a small simple village. It only feels like yesterday but it is a memory that grows fonder with every passing season. What he cannot accept is that he has changed. And he cannot bum around Peru anymore.

It's hard to admit but no matter how real and crusty

you think you are, you get used to the salary. And the mortgage. And the weekends. And even the moaning. And before you know it, it's ten years. An entire decade has passed.

And you still feel like you did when you were twenty-five, eighteen even. And you just can't work out what you're meant to be; young and free, or steady and responsible, so you try a bit of both. Mix and match.

We all play these little games with ourselves, and believe that we are unique. Different from the group, separate from the pack. But again we're not. I remember sitting in the pub after work one night with Tom, when our mutual wallowing and empty talk had become a little too much to bear.

So I asked him to take out his phone. And go through the names of his friends, one by one. And tell me what they do. And then tell me what they'd rather be doing.

And predictably, apart from the odd one or two, they almost all had these rather unfulfilling jobs, with uninspiring titles that give very little away.

Business development manager. Communications consultant. Strategic advisor. Network analyst. Project supervisor. Marketing this. Marketing that.

And equally predictably, they were almost all so much more talented, creative or interesting than their jobs. And they were all going to be something else.

Big dreams. Noble ideas. Important work. But they got sidetracked into their jobs. All of them. Fell into what they're doing. By accident. With the meter running and the years ticking by.

So it doesn't feel real. Their actual lives haven't begun

yet. What they're doing now is just a stop-gap. An in-between thing. It isn't really where they see themselves. They could all jack it in tomorrow. Start over.

Anytime soon. Which is just as well because there's no such thing as a job for life.

8: MOVIN' ON UP/I FEEL LIKE BUSTIN' LOOSE

When Quentin finally does call me into his office, I'm re-hydrated but tired and he seems more nervous than usual.

'I hear you boys had quite a night out on Friday,' he asks, trying to be down with the kids.

'Just a few drinks Quentin. Nothing special.'

'Tom says you kept him out all night. He looked pretty miserable this morning. He looks like he's been getting an earful from Ruth all weekend. He says you're a bad influence. Still you showed Ben a good time. I'll have to come along next time to show you a thing or two myself'

'Anytime Quentin.'

This is getting more awkward than usual. The bright strip-lighting is hurting my eyes and I want away quickly.

'So what did you want to see me about, Quentin? Is it that piece I wrote?'

'What?'

'The Torrid Media piece you emailed me about last week. Was it ok?'

'Yes, yes of course. I had a quick scan of it and Tom has sent it over to Philip at Torrid. Should be fine.'

He hasn't got a clue what I'm talking about, but blusters on.

'Good piece. Actually it's worked out well having

someone like you around as a dedicated resource. A scribe on the team. You've done a lot of valuable work, really added something to our capabilities with your writing.'

'Ok, thanks,' I say, immediately suspicious. I'm not at all sure where this is leading.

'I wanted to let you know that we've recognised your contribution. Your talents have been noted throughout the company.'

I'm getting confused. Quentin usually saves his pep talks for Tom or Gemma.

'That's really good to hear. Am I getting a raise?'

'No. No, erm actually it might be something better than that. Since coming to Silverback, you've become a really valuable asset to the company as a whole and it hasn't gone unnoticed. In fact, your name has been mentioned at a couple of board meetings recently. Even Dennis has been singing your praises and he thinks that you might be right for a new role that he has come up.'

'What, Dennis Squatter? I've hardly even spoken to him, are you sure he meant me?'

'Yes, he knows what a great job you've been doing with us and he liked what you did with the company brochure and website and thinks you might be right for something he has in mind.'

'What, copywriting for the whole company?'

'No, I think it might be something different, I don't have all the details but it sounds like an exciting opportunity. We don't want to lose you from the team but I'm really not going to stand in your way. I know that we couldn't hope to hold onto you forever and this sounds like it might be a good way of keeping you within the company.'

'Do you have any idea what it might be?'

'You'll have to speak to Dennis. But it sounds like the sort of thing that you really can't turn down and I just wanted to tell you that we'll be sorry to see you go but you have my complete blessings.'

I'm not sure I like the sound of this. This might suit Quentin more than me.

'What if I don't want to go, can I stay within the team?'

'Mmmm, well you see this might be a good move for everyone. You know what the market's been like recently and our operating costs are extremely high. It's becoming harder to justify having you as a dedicated copywriter in a small team like ours. We all value you extremely highly you know, but it can be difficult to explain having someone like you on the cost base to the other partners.'

'Ok, I see.'

'Listen why don't you talk to Dennis, he's very keen to see you get involved in this new project of his. This really could be an exciting opportunity for you, a chance to move up in the company.'

'Ok, I'll arrange a meeting with him and let you know what happens.'

'Excellent, excellent. That sounds like the best thing all round.'

Quentin is haunted by numbers. When he isn't out to lunch, he spends his entire time in his office, door shut, blinds down, locked in a frenzy of figures.

Adding up columns and taking away in ever more cryptic and senseless combinations.

Project work, expected earnings, the new business pipeline, fee re-negotiations all factored in each month in an attempt to inflate our figures.

Always trying to disguise the basic fact that we are losing clients and missing our targets, month after month.

It's hardly a secret. You can see it in his eyes at every team meeting he holds. White boards and marker pens. Dog-eared sandwiches cut into quarters. Defining our newest USP. Rehashing our latest business plan. Refining what we do over and over again. Glossing over our failures. Geeing up the troops.

And every month, like a lamb to the slaughter, he has to face up to the numbers and report to the board. The stern-eyed directors. God knows how he gets through it. His nervous, watery eyes and pale freckled skin only serve to accentuate his inner softness and his inability to face up to what the numbers are telling him.

So it sounds like all the talking may already have been done and I haven't really got much of a choice. No matter how valuable he says any of us are, in his world we've all been reduced to recurring digits on the balance sheet under outgoings and expenses.

But he just can't bring himself to sack anyone. He's so indecisive and he has this crippling desire to be liked. He can't even get rid of useless little Rhys, who has had numerous talkings to and untold final warnings.

Me moving on would be ideal. It'll ease the pain just a little bit. The best move for everyone. Writing on the wall, but happily for him no blood on the carpet.

I go back to my desk and call Dennis Squatter's PA. CEO, Silverback Business Communications. Feeling a little like a sacrificial lamb myself.

10: SHERYL CROW

There is an email from Tom. Torrid loved the piece. He wants to know if I can make it for a conference call to talk it through with Philip this afternoon.

I groan at the thought. Both Tom and I know that Philip loves being Philip. And he loves letting everyone know how great it is to be Philip.

He's a trend-bucker, a self-made man and a born leader. An aggressive alpha male who always knows his own mind and does things his way. Never shy of telling us how he takes on the odds and always wins.

Every day an anecdote. Some story that places him centre stage in a situation where his trusty insight allows him to see all the angles and do the unexpected. The renegade who flies by the seat of his pants only to come away by the skin of his teeth, unscathed and victorious. And always casually littered with references to famous shows or events, belittling them slightly to show that he's been there, done that, but hasn't been taken in by it.

And all of it related to the music industry. Although he actually runs a website design and technology company for whom the majority of clients are rather pedestrian. It is only PMC that links him to the more glamorous world of the music industry.

But then again most of our clients are telecoms and technology companies and we go on about Torrid. Philip may be our most awkward, volatile and irritating client but he is invariably mentioned whenever any of us are asked what we do for a living, simply because he still represents our one vicarious link to anything that sounds remotely sexy.

It's all relative, though. I get the distinct feeling that Philip is far from happy with his lot. He is a brash, abrasive man. One who steamrollers over all in his path. He is undoubtedly vain and self-serving, and a shameless revisionist, a mythmaker of epic proportion. But he seems restless, unsatisfied.

He has enormous energy, but like a hyperactive child his energy flies off in chaotic directions. He's always very passionate about the next new thing. Evangelical almost.

Sometimes it's sports. Often extreme. Boxing. Climbing. Hunting. Or speed. Motor-cycles. Sports cars. Track days. Whatever it is, Philip immerses himself utterly. As if he has something to prove, or needs to experience the jolt of something authentic to shake up the torpor of his existence. I'm not sure, he may simply be bored or it could be that he is looking for something, but if he is, his search seems random, unstructured, taking him into some improbable places.

He seeks out the company of those men who have mastered their discipline and who, in his mind, lead lives that are full of intense, rich experience. Men who in turn have learnt to master themselves in that moment of experience. He seeks them out and looks for their approval.

His latest thing is urban music, hardcore hip-hop. Gangsta flow from the ghettos of the US and grimy beats from UK estates. An unlikely choice. Comical in many ways. But again he's looking for genuine experience, that which is real, undiluted, uncut and raw. And like many white men, he feels the guilt that comes with his skin. Not of slavery. Or racism. But that of normalcy.

So having sat through the intensity of slipping a punch, or the sheer adrenaline of pushing the red line, we now have to endure Philip's newly found street slang, dress sense and urban attitude. Tom bears the brunt of it. But he's a client, he pays well and it's Tom's job to keep him happy.

Sitting in the conference room with Tom, both of us still slightly ashen-faced, my thoughts are still on the meeting with Quentin. I'll ask Tom what he thinks at the end of the call. He's good at politics. Works well within the system.

We both have printouts of the release I wrote in front of us. I quickly read it, remember what I've written and prepare myself for a barracking.

Tom dials in the number. Three rings and we're through to Philip's secretary.

Anna. Too tall. Too young. Too pretty. She could be Scandinavian, she could be Central European. She could be from the moon. She does look almost unreal. Like a different species here only to study the weaknesses of men. Middle-aged men.

Like Tom and myself.

The only way I can deal with her and keep some semblance of self-respect is not to react to her at all.

Pretend I haven't noticed. In the hope that this awkward, self-conscious play will mark me out as somehow so different to all the other hopefuls that drool for her attention. But somewhere, in the back of my mind, I know that even if this tactic worked and I managed, through some statistical error, to succeed and have her show some interest in me, I'd be paralysed by fear and over-analysis. I certainly wouldn't know what to do next and can't imagine myself enjoying it. Not even for a second.

She is almost a parody of the kind of woman Philip would hire as his PA. While his head of operations, who takes care of ninety percent of the running of Torrid, is a nervous, frayed-at-the-edges type, who obsesses about detail and makes a great play of how she puts up with Philip and takes care of him, Anna is pure bubblegum.

As soon as she speaks, I wonder what she's wearing.

'Sorry be right with you.'

Hold. Typically the music is operatic gangsta-rap.

'Torrid, Phil's office.'

'Hi Anna, It's Tom here from Silverback. We've got a conference call with Philip.'

Silence.

'Hello Anna…'

'Sorry, I wasn't listening. Who's that again?'

'Tom, from Silverback.'

'Who?'

'Tom from Silverback Business Communications'

Silence.

'We're your PR company. I was at your office last week.'

I imagine her staring into space.

'You came to our drinks party at Christmas.'

'Oh right. How can I help?'

'We've got a conference call with Philip.'

'Sorry he's not in the office. Can I take a message?'

'Are you sure? He emailed me twenty minutes ago asking us to call him.'

'Oh no that's right. He's been away somewhere. He just got back didn't he? I'm not sure if he's back yet, I've just got back from the gym. Let me check.'

She leaves the phone off the hook and we can hear her getting up and walking away from her desk. Tom looks at me, slightly red in the cheeks, but rolling his eyes, I shake my head.

'Just got back from the gym? It's four o' clock in the afternoon,' I whisper.

I'm interrupted by the sound of Anna's now distant voice shouting, echoing along the corridor to Philip's office.

'Phil are you there?'

'Oh hello. I didn't see you. How was the trip?'

'Really?'

'You never?'

'Did ya?'

'You're kidding.'

'And what did he say then?'

'You're joking me. Tell me you are. You are aren't ya?'

Both Tom and I now in stitches. We've hit the mute button on the conference phone but we can still hear one side of the conversation. Anna seems to have forgotten we are there.

I beg him not to but Tom eventually hangs up and calls Philip direct on his mobile.

'Philip, Tom here from Silverback, with Khaled. How was your trip?'

'Tom, nice one. Khaled how're you bro? I was just telling Anna. We've been at the World Musics. Dimepiece played the show, fucking sell-out. I tell you what though messy weekend Tom, very messy. Just flew in this afternoon. Had to take a later flight than planned. There was no way I was getting to the airport this morning. I was at the PMC party last night with the boys. Had a good chat with Max and Tony, the US veeps. Haven't a clue mate I tell ya. All the underground shit's coming out the tower-blocks and the council estates and these guys have still got fifty-year-old fat, fucking dinosaurs as head of A & R and marketing. I told them they need to build a street-team thing, guerrilla marketing, virals, stencils, info-pods but I might as well have been talking a different language, know what I mean?'

Neither Tom nor I have a clue what he's talking about. Tom bravely tries to change the subject.

'So how was the flight?'

'Don't know mate. Couldn't tell you. I was mullered. Slept through the whole thing. You should have seen the faces on all the other stiffs in first though. Looking at me like I'm some kinda kiddie fiddler prowling Toys R Us naah mean? I tell you what though, some fucking fascist tried to stop me at customs. Rass. Fucking little Hitler. He reckoned I was an illegal, or a fucking smuggler or something. Cheeky little twat.'

I dread to think what Philip would have looked like going through customs. Probably wearing a Public Enemy tour t-shirt, Cuban heels and a pimp fedora.

'So what happened Phil?' asks Tom.

'I just looked at him and told him that 'I fly first class all over the world mate and only in uptight little England is there ever a problem'. He didn't say nothing. Just carried on rooting through my bag, going through my dirty drawers 'n ting, and then when he couldn't find anything he starts staring at my passport. Like he's seen something dodgy. He says he's gonna have to run some checks. Do me a favour. I said, "Listen son. I employ fifty people in this country. Lived here all my life. I pay your wages. You know what, I probably pay three or four times what you earn in tax to this Babylon country and this how I get treated." He couldn't say nothing after that. Had to let me go about my business.'

We hear a strange sound, which I realise is Philip sucking his teeth indignantly, I chase the image of rubber gloves from my mind and take my chance to break in.

'Hey Philip. Khaled here. Sounds like a nightmare, I hope he didn't keep you too long, but listen we don't want keep you, especially if you're running late today. You wanted to talk about the Cruzin' piece I wrote, was it alright? No problems I hope'

'Hey Khaled, yeah man, whassup bro? Yeah just a fascist with a badge and uniform, I know you're feeling me dawg, you know what it's like. Yeah that piece. No problems. Bo! Loved it man. 'Chief Strategic Tinkerer'. Classic. And genius headline. 'Torrid number ones', you're telling me man. I tell ya. Just a coupla ting 'n ting though. I need my quote to be a little higher up, it can't be on the second page, and I got some feedback from those muppets at PMC, you can't call Cruzin' a boy-band, they've had what like five hundred number ones or summit, innit? They shift units man. Cashing large cheques and making mo' cheddar and you can't beat that. Not even with a baseball bat. No you have to refer to them as major league recording artists. It's contractual.'

We wind down the call and leave the room. I decide against speaking to Tom about meeting with Quentin because it's dawning on me that a change might do me good.

11: THE WHEELS OF INDUSTRY

Silverback Financial Public Relations was set up in the mid-80s by a group of bright, aggressive, and extremely well-connected ex-public-school boys who had all done their round in the City.

It was a time when Greed was Good and even Del-boy started to wear red braces. Our parents had already begun to invest in property but then decided they could all make money out of thin air by dabbling in shares.

I can remember my Dad joining the very British rush to buy British Telecommunications, British Gas, British Steel, all of which was supposed to belong to us anyway, but most of all I remember the day he finally got rid of our dilapidated old Sony so he could check his portfolio on Teletext.

The guys at Silverback rode the wave, selling stories about FTSE 100 companies into the nationals and organising journalist and analyst meetings, results and AGMs, helping to market the Square Mile to a country desperate to cash in.

Silverback did well. Really well. It grew to thirty people.

And then it doubled. It picked up more clients eager to reach the savings of hopeful families up and down the country. It started to move into new areas: investor relations, investor roadshows, opening up the provinces. It continued to grow. More City types joined alongside washed up ex–journalists.

And then it got bought out by a faceless American media conglomerate, eager to establish a foothold in London, the key to the unexploited, newly deregulated financial markets of the UK and Europe.

Silverback's founders became millionaires many times over on paper. Some cashed in while others continued to live the fat cat dream. America caught a cold, there were ripples in the Far East, markets crashed, property crashed, negative equity. Savings lost, houses repossessed.

Belts were tightened, jobs were lost but Silverback continued to do well. Crisis management, corporate PR, media relations. It went from Silverback Financial PR to Silverback Business Communications. It was sold again. More American dollars flowed in, insulating the already very rich men at Silverback even further.

Technology suddenly became interesting. Technology suddenly became sexy. Computers. Communications. Convergence. Email and the Internet. Dotcom explosion. Mobile phones. WAP. Sky Digital. M&As, IPOs, seed funds and venture capital. Nasdaq, Techmark, Boo.com. Money for nothing. New fortunes to be made.

Again Silverback caught the wave. Two hundred people, offices around the world. Brand extension. Expense accounts and acquisition vehicles. A sense of empire. Delusions of grandeur. Invincibility.

But the fragile, ephemeral bubble burst again. Global

advertising budgets slashed. Media conglomerates shedding staff. Downsizing. Cost-cutting.

And then one day a bean-counter in New York noticed that Silverback, always a steady earner, a good cash cow, had become extremely top-heavy. Full of millionaires with double-barrelled names. Cavalier men with a taste for the high life and no intentions of weaning themselves off.

Meetings were called. Transatlantic videoconferences held. Excessive entertainment was mentioned. Golf days for clients. Rows of tickets at Wimbledon. Grand Prix's and Rugby. First class travel. Five star hotels. And the final nail in the coffin, a hunting weekend in Wiltshire that came in at over at thirty grand.

Silverback's corpulent alpha-male simply had to go. And his number two. Decisive action. A purge at the top. Management cull. Restoring investor confidence. Shaking out the deadwood. Fifth Avenue had spoken, Fifth Avenue was obeyed.

It all happened so quickly, none of us in the office knew a thing about it till it was all over and the company email went out. Reassuring us that all was well. Change was good. Change was necessary. Onwards and upwards again. Mutually agreed terms. Everybody happy. Everybody smile.

We all pretended to panic a little. But really we relished the distraction. Wild rumours flew about. Talk of a management buyout. Talk of job losses. Talk of a new Silverback being set up by the old guard. But it all came to nothing. Everything settled down. We all carried on as before, hardly aware of the change.

And so it came to pass that Dennis Squatter MBA took over the reins at Silverback.

A new broom. Full of big ideas. Full of nervous energy. Big on management technique. Ready to strengthen ties with the mothership.

At his introductory, 'get to know the gang' meeting, none of us really understood what he was talking about. But we all laughed and nodded and clapped on cue.

At the lectern, he reminded me of an overactive chimpanzee, or a scruffy little schoolboy who simply can't stand still. Constantly fiddling with something. Constantly fiddling with himself. Picking at his cuffs, readjusting his trousers or pushing and pulling his wire-framed glasses up and down the bridge of his sharp little nose.

He made me nervous. I think he made us all nervous. Most of us shuffled out to the free beer and wine that followed and hardly ever saw him again, while others pressed forwards, eager to make themselves known and please our new leader.

After that initial meeting, there was a flurry of activity. We learned that knowledge management was his thing. Knowledge mining. Tapping intellectual property and sharing it enterprise-wide.

A special working group was set up. Extremely inclusive, with people from every tier of the company. We were all encouraged to speak our minds. From a top-down perspective, mind you.

New working methods were introduced. We all had to attend seminars and training meetings before and after work to assess what we do and to define our attainment needs. Invest in knowledge, invest in people. People are our number one asset. I wrote a new brochure and website. Some of us even got shiny new laptops and fancy new phones.

And all too soon, we all began to resent geeky Dennis Squatter MBA and his interfering ways. Even the ones with the new laptops. Even the ones who had rushed forwards to greet him. We all groaned together every time he emailed us with a new piece of revolutionary thinking or the latest must-read article.

But no one said anything directly to him, no one resisted.

Instead, we all acquiesced to Dennis. And he carried on bounding around the office, in and out, busy, busy, convinced that we were all in it together, pulling in the same direction, reading from the same hymn sheet.

One happy, tight-knit little group.

12: FAITH

There is an old joke, not a very good one, about a suicidal man on Christmas Eve, who meets Father Christmas just as he's about to jump off a bridge. Santa asks him what's wrong, and the man replies that his wife has left him for another man and taken his kids. He's lost his job through drinking and depression and his house has just been repossessed and he can't face Christmas in that state. Father Christmas tells him not to jump. Tells him wait till Christmas morning and go back to his house. His wife will be back, there'll be presents under the tree for his children. A perfect domestic scene and everything back to normal.

The man is beside himself with joy and gratitude and

feels he must repay Father Christmas in some way. 'Anything, anything at all, you name it.'

After some cajoling Father Christmas says, 'There is just one thing you could do, it may seem a little strange. Are you sure you want to do it?'

'I'll do it. Whatever it is. I'll do it.'

'Ok take these,' says Father Christmas. 'Handcuff yourself to the railing and drop your trousers.'

The man is shocked but agrees to do it, such is the extent of his gratitude.

'Just one thing,' says Father Christmas. 'Aren't you a little old to believe in Christmas?'

A corny joke, but that's all it is. Just a joke. Not the sort of thing that could ever really happen.

The thing is though, there's a court case going on at the moment. A very human story. The kind of thing that sends the media into a frenzy, allowing the tabloids to revel in the lurid details and the broadsheets to sermonise about the lamentable state of our modern times.

At the centre of the scandal is a man, in his mid-fifties. Rather undistinguished in appearance. Badly-dyed, boot-polish hair brylcreemed over a bald spot. Thick, plastic-framed glasses that grossly distort the look of his eyes. Blue naval blazers, buttons missing, tatty, worn, sprinkled with dandruff. A heavy paunch, accentuated by a high waistband, the way they used to wear their trousers. Scrawny wrists and neck. An altogether shabby and disproportionate figure of a man.

Yet this man was kept by a harem of women. All of them younger by at least a decade. And attractive. Relatively speaking. He made homes with these women country-wide. He broke up marriages, fathered children. He took money. Travelled constantly. Kept it up for just over three years. Until he got careless, and somehow revealed the existence of one of his other women to a previously trusting and kind-hearted lady, who sought vengeance with a formidable zeal, devoting herself entirely to uncovering the extent of his deceit.

When caught, the man is said to have expressed relief. He could no longer go on living a lie. Whereas his women could no longer go on living without it.

I've followed the case religiously, which is appropriate really. It turns out that after a lifetime of petty conniving, this man hit upon his one defining scam, a no-frills effective con. And it happened completely by accident.

It started in a church. He was at the time, leading a near transient life. On the scrounge. He was only ever in church when it was cold outside because the flop-house where he slept turfed people out for the day. He'd been eyeing the collection box for several weeks, until finally, seeing his opportunity to swoop one morning after the service was over and the thin congregation scattered, he made his move.

He snuck back into the church before the gates had been locked and made his way to a cold anteroom, where he started his fruitless search for the collection box.

It was during his bungling search that he was discovered by a church volunteer, who had come back to lock up. By chance, the same kindly lady who would later spearhead such an effective single-handed campaign for justice and revenge.

Upon seeing the man, she rightly demanded who he

was and what he was doing there. Our man, no master-criminal, panicked and said the first thing that came into his head. 'Billy Graham,' he said, 'I'm Billy Graham, Yes I'm Billy Graham. I'm in England on a secret visit. You mustn't tell. I'm Billy Graham.'

And she believed him.

It wasn't so much the fact that his story was watertight. He would later refine it and add props and accoutrements, but he was never really that plausible.

Of course it helped that he yelped out a name that we all recognise but belongs to a face that most of us don't.

I've often thought that this must be a rich vein for more accomplished con-artists; I remember a story about one man in the States who sustained a long career out of claiming he was Redhead Kingpin, a long-retired, one-hit-wonder of a rapper, best known for the colour of his hair. But people half-remembered the name so he was booked to appear on the college circuit in the Southern states, apparently giving great shows, once he'd rattled through the Kingpin's rather limited back catalogue.

And then I seem to recall the case of a woman who claimed she was the soul singer Martha Reeves of the Vandelas. She appeared on TV several times on local network chat shows, where she was an entertaining and revealing guest, although suspiciously youthful looking. She was always reluctant to sing but was on occasion persuaded to perform live in front of a studio audience, who didn't really know who she was supposed to be but applauded anyway despite her lack of any discernable vocal talent.

And these are just the cases of the people who got caught. The ones I can remember. There must be a whole legion of pranksters and conmen out there who have cottoned onto the potency of brand recognition that a well-known name can generate, especially when coupled with an anonymous face.

It's even occurred to me when I'm locked in a lie. I reckon impersonating an author would be good sport. We all vaguely know their names, and are reluctant to admit that we don't actually read. And who really knows what these strange and solitary birds are supposed to look like anyway.

But back to our Billy Graham impersonator. A man singularly lacking in physical charms or any overt charisma. A degree of cheap cunning, but no criminal genius. Yet he persuaded many, many otherwise stable and secure women to believe in him. To take him in. To part with money. He convinced these Christian ladies to support the ministry in other ways, to fulfil the very specific needs and requirements of the man at its centre. To suspend not only their disbelief but also their personal and much-prized morality. Not only living in sin, but allowing perhaps the twin sins of vanity and pride to skew their judgement.

And I wonder why? I can only guess but I imagine he imparted a special gift to each of his victims. A certain understanding was reached. And fair exchange is no robbery.

He chose them out of a crowd. He made them part of an intrigue that added some spice to their lives. Granted, after the first time, he picked his marks to suit his scam; pious women for whom access to the gateway to heaven could be fast-tracked through good connections here on earth. But even so there was no real reason for them to believe. They just did.

Remember our man is English, speaks with an English accent, looks nothing like Billy Graham, and was supposedly on a secret reconnaissance trip to the UK for over three years in order to extend his franchised ministry.

But none of these ladies ever checked up on him. His bubble only burst through his own incompetence. He really wasn't any kind of master criminal at all, and he only stumbled upon Billy Graham, through sheer chance.

Had he been a real artist, he would have said he was Father Christmas.

13: LUBRICATION

Dennis still makes me nervous. He never seems to finish any of his sentences. And he has some disconcerting personal habits that make it difficult to retain eye contact. Blowing his nose on his tie. Tearing the corners off notepads and using the paper to clean between his teeth.

Maybe it's a deliberate ploy. The walls of his office are lined with those international business best sellers that share with us gems such as the seven previously unknown habits of highly effective people.

Perhaps he's testing out some radical piece of research from one of his books: 'How to gain the upper hand in a meeting and keep your opponent off-balance through farting, belching and picking your teeth.'

He does all of that and more in his meeting with me, during which he spends most of the time checking his emails and taking 'important' calls.

And he doesn't know my name. He keeps calling me Karim. It's all very tragic, as I don't correct him at my first and only opportunity.

'How do you feel about the new challenge Karim? Up for it?'

'Actually I'm not sure what it is yet.'

'The digital age Karim. That's the only game in town,' he says, swivelling round in his chair and throwing his arms wide open from his scrawny body as if he's rehearsing giving a keynote speech in front of an audience of his rapturous peers. 'It's the future. Our shared future. And it's already upon us. Are you ready for it? Are you ready for the future?'

His voice drops to a near whisper. He pauses to cue his killer-line. He looks directly into my eyes to ensure emotional buy-in and goes for the payoff.

'Are you ready for the future now, Karoosh?'

'Err, I think..'

'Yes you are Karrrrerm, yes you are,' his voice rising, as his eyes shift back to his screen. 'You're a switched on young man. You understand that technology is the key. You are the new wave, pushing forwards. The envelope, yes the leading edge. Pushing through. To the other side.'

He stops cold, as confused as me by what he has just said, but he quickly rallies and manages to push on.

'We need people like you to drag Silverback forwards. Kicking and screaming if needs be.'

'Yes Dennis, what exactly do you have in mind?'

He swivels in his chair to face me again, fiddling maniacally with his glasses. 'Great things Karim. Great things. I need people like you with me. Are you with me?'

'Err yes, I ..'

'Good, good. That's what I like to hear. You see, Silverback, is like a big engine. Lots of cogs and gears. Interlocking, all vital. Working together, moving, unison, in unison, yes, forwards, meshing together.'

His words have started to trip into each other, as again he appears to work himself up into a twitchy fit. His eyes are glassy, and I feel as if I could almost slip away unnoticed.

'And I'm the engineer,' he pauses for a moment as if pleased by this new thought. "I look at the whole machine. I tweak and I twiddle. Order new parts. Tighten the screws, fix any leaks. Keep it ticking over smoothly and uhmm, headed in the right direction. Mmmm yes purring along. Smoothly. Like a big cat. A big, beautiful, ferocious cat.'

'Yes, and how do I fit in?' I ask with increasing alarm.

'Oil and grease Karim, oil and grease.'

'I'm sorry?'

'You are the oil, Karim. You are the grease. Oil for the engine to keep the gears from grinding. To keep the cat purring. I know you understand the business, but you stand slightly outside of it, so you're uhmm, not a cog or a gear, you see.'

Just as I think he has blown himself out, he picks up a new thread and takes off again mumbling breathlessly. 'And I know you understand technology, the benefits. You get to the core of it immediately, see past all the window dressing. That's why I need you. Yes, I need you to be the oil for a new project. I need you to feed the cat. Lubricate it, so it slots smoothly into the Silverback machine.'

'So what do you need me to do?' I say over him. Both our voices rising in this airless little fishbowl office. I'm trying to talk over him to make him stop.

'That's what I like to hear Kerrrumm, Kerrrr yes that's right, enthusiasm. Can do. This is a great opportunity for you, a real step up,' he says shouting yet louder.

His eyes are darting round the room and he is now busily dismantling a biro. 'We're taking on the digital age. Grasping the ummm …grasping it with both hands. You know how? Karrrr… do you know how?'

I shake my head at him, careful not to look at the sticky blue mess that now covers his hands and trousers. I'm getting short of breath.

I think I might be having an anxiety attack.

'I'll tell you, Kareesh. Let me tell you. We are going to build it together. You and I. We're going to take it on. We going to stare into the void and we're going to master it. Aren't we Khalil?'

"Yes. I mean no. I mean I don't understand. What do you want me to do sir?" My head is spinning. I feel frenzied and confused.

"We're going to make an… extranet,' he sinks back into his seat, with a sigh, a dreamy look in his eye and a satiated glow to his face.

I feel as if I should say something; something that shows my awe and gratitude. But I stay silent and feel nothing but a creeping nausea at the thought that I've been violated in some unseen way.

Dennis is lying back in his chair, he flicks a lever and it tilts back to near horizontal. He seems to be staring sightlessly at the ceiling, licking his lips.

I can now see the hairy gap, between his Walt Disney socks and his frayed turn-ups. His shiny trousers have bunched up around his crotch.

His voice is now a low murmur. I can only catch every other word or phrase. 'Linking it through to the website... feeding it all through... backend... knowledge management... Seamless. Beautiful... just beautiful.'

I'm not sure what this all means or what I'm supposed to say. I hear a strange voice that's not my own, strangle out something like: 'Extranet, sir. Fantastic sir. I couldn't agree more sir. Do you want me to find a design agency sir, I've worked with Torrid sir, they're a client sir, I've worked with them sir. I have sir.'

He turns his head slowly towards me, I can see a shiny line of spittle, drooling towards his chin. He wipes at it, leaving a blue smear across his lips. I feel horrified. 'No need,' he says. 'We have all the capabilities in-house. We'll use our IT guys. Tap into their knowledge. Involve the designers. Get them together and let's rock and roll.'

'Yes sir, great idea sir, totally agree, sir.' By now I'll say anything to get out of there.

He lurches forwards towards me, his hand outstretched. I jump up to my feet, not sure of his intentions. But all he wants is to do, is give me the power-shake.

14: PEST CONTROL

Our building is being fumigated. The pest-controllers have turned up with poisons and masks. Canisters of gas and heavy-duty gloves. What look like traps and baits.

But no one knows why they're here. It's not clear what we're supposed to be infested with.

They were called in by the building managers. The building managers claim there was an emergency request from our office manager. Our office manager says she received an emergency order to evacuate the building from the building managers. At very late notice. Barely time to inform the staff and rearrange meetings.

Confusion reigns. Recriminations. Phone calls are made. Explanations demanded. The partners are not happy. Not happy at all. Dennis looks on. He's fascinated by the equipment.

He picks up a sprayer that's been set down while things are being sorted out and starts to fiddle with the sinister looking nozzle, pointing it directly towards his eye. Squinting. Looking right at it. Finger dangerously close to the trigger. Until he's noticed by a gruff looking pest-control technician with rock-and-roll sideburns and an impressive pompadour, and told to put it down. Immediately. Which he does. Red-faced. Twitchy.

A senior person from the management company turns up. He's got printouts of emails in his hands. From us to him.

Our office manager denies ever sending them. She quickly counters with faxes of her own. They eye each other suspiciously. And then the senior building manager man shows us why he's the senior man. He points out that the faxes sent to us are on the correct fax paper etc etc, but they've been sent from the local copy centre. It's clearly visible in small print at the head of every faxed page.

Our office manager demands to look again at the emails that have been sent from her email account. And notices a small difference in the name of the sender. Her email address has a dot in it separating first name from second. The email address that is printed out on the senior building manager's paper trail does not.

Again he shows his worth. Shaking his head in a knowing way.

'What is it?' asks our office manager, clearly out of her depth.

'Can't you tell?' asks the senior building manager. 'Disgruntled employee. Clear case.'

I feel hot and guilty. But it wasn't me. I just wish it had been and have to wonder if it shows on my face.

'Want us to give you a once over anyway? As we're here like,' asks the gruff looking Elvis fan in the boiler suit.

15: PUSHERMAN

Tom and I are at it again. Drinking red wine when we should be at home. Just before six his resolve weakened, early in the week and he asked me if I fancied getting together for a quick one after work.

He knows something is up. As Quentin's right hand, he probably had some prior knowledge but no real details. And the rumours have already started.

I'd been seen in Quentin's office and then in Dennis'

and the talk soon followed. Rhys and Gemma forming a hasty alliance to share intrigue and opinion. Rhys even making a clumsy attempt to engage me in pally conversation.

I'm surprised at the attention, but we're all a little bit bored I suppose. Other than the fact they might see something in it for themselves, either an opportunity to advance or a chance to vent some frustration, I don't really see why any one of them should care at all about what's happening to me. Office gossip I guess.

It's simply a distraction, a break in the monotony, and one that serves to illustrate how bad things are in our desperate little team. When we're chugging along, we just accept and get on with it, but when an event gives us pause for thought, forcing us to examine ourselves and our relative position within the group, we have to acknowledge how awful the dynamic really is.

So as long as the issue remains unsettled and things are up in the air, we'll have paranoia, grumbling and chatter. Which is why Tom wants to get to grips with things quickly.

He is far more decisive and capable than Quentin, who instinctively leaves things for Tom to sort out. While some people insist that training and technique build management skill, it is in fact empathy and a human touch, which Tom has naturally in abundance.

He takes his time before broaching the subject. We talk instead about quitting Silverback as usual, leaving an open segue point for me to step through.

I resist for a while, and talk as if nothing is different, but Tom is patient. No pressure. He just lets me talk. It's difficult to hold out any enthusiasm for the deception with Tom. It takes two for that relationship to work. Sure, I could simply feed him inaccuracies, factual errors and misinformation, but you need somebody who will bite; a reaction of some kind, a change of behaviour that you have authored for any real satisfaction.

No Tom is too measured. Calm. He sees all sides and hears all the voices. Understands where people are coming from. And he won't rush. Not himself or those that he's dealing with.

So eventually I break off my holding pattern and tell him my news and ask what he thinks.

'Quentin said something about Dennis wanting you for a new job, but I didn't know what. Have you thought it through, I mean it sounds a bit sketchy, what does he expect you to do exactly?'

'Tom, to be honest with you, I don't really know what he wants. Or why he chose me. But it's a neat little solution: he wants someone to work on his pet project and Quentin needs to get rid of someone.'

Tom says nothing. A familiar trick. He'll gain more by listening than by spouting off. But for once I'm not buying it: I just don't feel the need to have him take my side and strangely, I don't really want to let off steam either.

'Tom. It is what it is. I can take it or leave it. My choice in the end.'

'Well yeah. You're right. Ok.'

Another pause.

'When you make up your mind, we can think about what you want to tell the others,' he says.

'I know you don't like Rhys and Gemma or Ben not

knowing, but really, what's it to do with them? What's it matter what they think?' I ask, feeling a little annoyed, that I'm not at the centre of his thinking.

'It's just good for people to know what's going on.'

I can sense him bracing himself for an attack but I can't muster the energy. I am resigned to the fact that change has been forced upon me.

Instead I ask him something else. Perhaps to distract myself.

'Don't worry Tom, I understand. I'll let you know as soon as I decide. We can't keep them waiting and gossiping forever. But just think about it for a second; there are so many ways we could break the news you know? We could say anything. We could have a field day. Especially with Rhys. Don't you think?'

Again Tom waits for me to go on. He won't even want to bad-mouth Rhys, which is a common sport, without hearing more from me and getting the lay of the land first. I'm beginning to feel quite cheated, which is why I carry on, wanting to bait him into saying something.

'I could tell him whatever I want. He's so eager to hear something right now. He's primed and ready; he'd lap it up. Asking for it really. Almost a shame not to give him what he wants'

'What would be the point of that?' asks Tom warily.

'I don't know. Just for fun I guess. Just to see how far I could push it. You know what I mean. Don't you ever wonder how far you could take something like that? Just to see?'

'Not really, Khaled. It's not the sort of thing that gets me going.'

Something in the teacherly tone of his voice makes me quite unwilling to drop it now. So I keep pushing. Just a little further. To get that reaction.

'Don't come the innocent Tom. You could easily do it. You know you could.'

'Yeah I could, but why would I want to? It wouldn't be difficult to lie to someone. Especially someone like Rhys, so what's the point?'

'No that's exactly it. That's the reason right there. You said it yourself. "Someone like Rhys." You're right he's easy. He so anxious and so blocked up, he wants to be told something. He's waiting for it. You'd almost be doing him a favour. And whatever the lie is he'll twist it round, and make it fit into his own little view of the world. He'll make it true.'

'Yeah so what does that prove? Rhys is a bit fucked-up. We all know that. There's no need to go on about it. It might make him a bit vulnerable or a bit gullible. And I know he can be a pain, but still that's no excuse. It'd be like picking on someone who's smaller than you.'

'No, you're right, it would be. But you're missing my point Tom. I'm not saying pick on someone easy just because you can. I'm saying I wonder how far you could take it. Not just Rhys. You're right it's obvious with him. He's fucked up. But there must be something for everyone. Something that will make them want to believe.'

'Well yeah. Everyone's got a weak spot. We all like to think we're not gullible but it just depends. It's all about pushing the right buttons I guess.'

I wonder if I may have pushed some of Tom's. His voice has a little more feeling to it. A touch of irritation, which suddenly has the blood pumping a little faster.

'Yeah maybe, I don't know. But that's not what I mean. What I'm saying is. Once you know what it is. Whatever it may be. And the person is swallowing what you're telling them. I just wonder how far could you push it.'

'You know what mate? You're beginning to sound like one of these wierdos now, Khaled. You know, one of those people whose neighbours say, "Oh I didn't really know him. He kept himself to himself. But he seemed like such a nice polite young man,' says Tom laughing, a little tightly perhaps. 'Just what is it you'd get people to do?'

'No mate, you don't understand. Lying to people is easy. You said it yourself. Getting them to do what you want probably isn't that difficult either. I mean if you have enough conviction and sincerity, you can get them to believe what you say and get them to act on it. No, the thing I'm talking about is, how far can you really take it? I mean, could you lie to someone, get them hooked? Get them believing in something because they want to, for whatever reasons they have of their own, and then tell them it was all a lie? Would they listen to you then or would they just want to keep believing the lie that they've made their own?"

Tom is looking at me. Silent again. The thought I've just expressed is new to me. Maybe something that doesn't sound so good out loud. A little intense, or perhaps just weird like he says.

I've pushed and prodded perhaps a bit too far. I fall silent and look away from Simon's face. I reach for the bottle of wine that sits empty on the table between us. I put it back down and attempt to pull myself back over the line.

'Listen mate, I don't know what I'm going on about. Just talking shit. You know I've got a lot on my mind at the moment and I just need to stop thinking about it and make a decision. I'll let you know as soon as I do. The way I'm feeling, I'll probably give it a go. I may not have much choice but you know it may be a good thing. I could do with a change. Yeah, I'll probably give it a go. See what happens, hey? But I'll definitely let you know as soon as I know what I'm doing.'

16: ASK THE DUST, CRAB-KILLER

Dennis' big project. A total nightmare from start to early finish. Our Chief Engineer certainly talks a good game. And he definitely left his mark on me. It took me two days to scrub away the last traces of blue ink he smeared across my hand.

He takes his cues from *Management Today*, *The Wall Street Journal* and Harvard Business School. Heroic visionary thinking, laid out in tough bombastic words. I've read the articles. They're all very do or die. But short on detail.

And when I look to Dennis for direction or even a practical brief of some kind it becomes apparent that he has no idea what any of this involves. Neither do I.

My team is no help either. A couple of sullen IT support staff that talk in impenetrable code, and then moan that no one understands what they do. And two designers who both wish they were working in an advertising agency or a fashionable magazine, rather than being asked to produce crappy covers for reports and corporate brochures.

They are nothing but delinquent attitude; overgrown

boys who refuse to grow up. And like all boys they like to bully. They try to intimidate me. Again unwilling to share the precious secrets of their trade. Precious. Haughty. Difficult. Little princes who look down at people who do not share their obsessive minority interests.

And at the bottom of the pyramid there is Sammie, a young, awkward, put-upon assistant. Very pale skin. Shy. Uninspired. Clumsy. Quiet. A shoe-gazer.

All of us stuck at the end of corridor next to the stationary cupboard, opposite the photocopiers. From little acorns. Yeah right.

An invisible team of backroom support staff misfits. I soon realise why I've been asked to do the job. No one else in the company would take it. I wasn't the first to be asked. In fact I wasn't really asked at all. And when they tried to hire someone in to do the job, they couldn't find anyone for less than sixty-five grand a year.

And the job soon becomes scaled down; all of it put on the back-burner in less than a month, when it becomes apparent that there is no budget, a total lack of skills and complete resistance from everyone within the company.

So I'm left in charge of the photocopying and PC-crash crew. Dennis tells me it's an opportunity. Open-ended. Tap into their skills. Unlock their potential. Lead them into new areas.

He says that he wishes that it were him in my shoes. Just before he forgets all about us. He's onto his next new project, something about producing video broadcast releases for our clients. Apparently it's the future of PR.

So here I am in complete limbo. I have absolutely nothing to do any more. No role to perform. Quentin won't take me back and if I kick up too much of a fuss with Dennis I could end up losing my job.

I'll have to keep turning up and try to look busy. Sounds ideal but very soon the novelty wears off and the boredom kicks in.

And there is a particular grinding texture to the boredom I endure in the silence of an office in which I have become an employment zombie. I just turn up to pick up my pay and sit silent for days on end.

I remember those long colourless afternoons of unemployment where the enemy was loneliness. Loneliness that comes from the fear of facing people who might guess what you are.

Now there is nowhere to hide away. I'm highly visible and exposed on all sides, but I'm still as cut off as ever from the moist, warm bodies that breathe the same air as me.

Minutes turn to treacle. I sit and wait. Breakfast runs. Email checking. Mid-morning coffee. Newspapers. The joy of lunch, which you put back as long as possible, so it will eat into the afternoon. Toilet breaks. Popping round to see people you don't really like to say hello. Anything that takes you away from the prison of your desk. And then just watching the clock, waiting until someone speaks, or someone leaves so you can follow.

There have been other times when the task in hand has been so brutally mindless and repetitive, I have managed to escape my physical body to daydream away the hours. Sometimes the technique of the job itself can even become a focus for abstraction, so that every bag of sawdust I stuffed or plate I washed would become a triumphant masterpiece in itself.

But even this becomes an impossibility when your days are utterly blank. A boredom discount factor comes into effect, proving that everything is always entirely relative. I crave the solace of people and conversations that I would normally walk to other side of the road to avoid. And find myself reading story after story from a vast array of news sources on the internet, not so much to absorb the information, more to simply give myself a task that takes up some time.

I wander aimlessly around, lost on the web, clicking one link after the next, searching for something to amuse. I download music that I'll never listen to again, disks and disks of it. I've become an obsessive collector, trying to capture and catalogue something that I know will never be complete. I shop online and take part in auctions for obscure junk. I've signed up to numerous alerts, desperate for the trivia and the amusement that I've always scorned others for seeking out and wasting their time on.

But worst of all I've become a pest, because I share each minute detail of every last thing I'm up to. The type of person who interrupts others who are trying to work. Who starts off stories that have no end, or middle, or any meaning at all. I hover when others are talking. I butt in and I jar the nerves of those upon whom I have imposed my presence. I've even attempted to write one of those stupid emails that you hope will be passed on from person to person around the world.

And then there are other things that I do that border on the bizarre. Little jolts of anarchy inspired by the pest controller. Minor stuff that alleviates the unyielding nature of the day. I never flush when I've gone to the loo, leaving a little surprise for the next person who happens along. I steal a page out of every newspaper that sits in the common room. I readjust people's seats and the height of the screens. I misfile documents and return folders upside down and out of sequence in the shared archive. I take things from desks and leave them elsewhere. Whenever someone is away from their desk, I leave them voicemails that are garbled, unclear, but mention their names. And their client names. I leave cryptic messages on whiteboards, in meeting rooms and on photocopiers all over the building. Little nonsensical pieces of surreal poetry, that mean nothing but scream insanity.

But I know I have a shadow. Someone more prolific and inventive than even myself. He is the arch prankster, who works on a grand and daring scale. His is a sustained campaign that has gone largely unnoticed but has targeted us all. And he now has a name.

We were all sent a beautifully wrapped empty box, marked with the name Arturo B. We opened it and cast it aside, vaguely disappointed at the thought of yet another pointless teaser campaign.

Several weeks later a desk calendar arrived, again marked Arturo, completely plain, but instead of marking the days of the week, it only showed the weekends, two weeks in August and the week from Christmas to New Year. The rest of the year completely blank. Again, no one really paid any attention; we looked at it in the morning, wondered what it was all about and forgot all about it by lunchtime.

Other little strange things kept happening but nothing you'd link together as part of a campaign, unless you know he's out there. I noticed a small sign buried on the noticeboard, alongside all the dated appeals for removals men, good plumbers in South London and details of people looking for non-smoking flatmates with GSOH to move in with. It simply said 'Help Wanted', signed AB.

Little labels from a Letraset started appearing around the office, in meeting rooms, in the kitchen and on people's desks, saying cryptic things like 'Bankrupt', 'My Other Car's a Ferret' and 'Work makes us free'. Stickers appeared in the lift next to the buttons and the display saying things like 'Floor 2 and half — sort of in between' or 'Going Down, Down, Down' or 'Now wash your hands'.

And then there are other things that continue to happen on an occasional basis that target specific people. Several of the partners, including Quentin, received gold embossed invitations to attend a gala dinner and awards show from DBX, the Directorate of Business Excellence, but when asked to RSVP on their behalf, their secretaries found themselves dialling a premium rate gay chat number called DIRTBOX.

Nothing's happened to me as yet, but just last week the Corporate Property team returned from a team lunch to find their screensavers set to a picture of an unknown black footballer. It was only the next day that they realised that their email signatures had been changed to read Arturo Blisset.

Nothing's happened to me yet, but I'm keeping my eyes and ears open. I wonder if Arturo, whoever he is, has noticed my own little acts of sedition. I can't imagine who he could be, but he has become a guiding light; I'd love to know what he thinks of my work even though I know I'm nowhere near his league. But even so, some acknowledgement would be nice. I imagine what it'd be like if we could work together, but there's simply no way either one of us can make ourselves known.

We'll each simply have to continue as autonomous cells of bored resistance, each of us doing what we can and making sure we don't get caught. But at least knowing that he exists, someone just like me, gives me hope, while searching for signs of his passing and clues to his identity helps break up the monotony of these fallow days.

17: LE PATRON EST FOU

Today is the first day of the rest of my life.

I've been ghost-walking for far too long. It's beginning to affect me. I'm regressing, turning into a shadow. At work I've gone days without speaking more than ten words to another soul.

And at home I just lock myself in my room, not sleeping because in my mind sleep has become the cousin of death. Instead I stay awake smoking weed every night with the door shut, making the entire flat smell stale. I sit there alone ignoring Jun when he comes to my door, asking me to turn the music down.

I'm so tired. My eyes are permanently red. And my skin is turning grey. Hanging from my sides. Fatty pouches from ice cream and salty snacks from strip-lit convenience stores at one in the morning.

My cough is deep and bubbling. I can't get hard, or even muster the energy to masturbate. But the thing that finally shakes me out of my haze is when I see blood in the toilet bowl after two days of constipation.

I have to pull myself together. This can't go on.

I know that work has been dragging me down, and so, I decide to meet the problem head on. I must throw myself into work. Throw myself into my team. With zeal and enthusiasm. For my own sake.

They are taken aback to say the least. Unresponsive. Resentful. Aggressive. Feathers all ruffled up. Squawking noise at me.

Whispering behind my back.

But there can't be any turning back because I know that my melancholy hasn't gone far. It's waiting patiently in the wings, keeping my dark thoughts company. They take a ticket and wait for their number to come up once again. The sticky green weed offers a helping hand. The red wine and vodka send me a postcard. Wish you were here?

And I know myself. I'm so very easily bored. Like a child. Disruptive. And distracted. I need something to keep me interested and amused.

It isn't going to be easy. I'm totally unsuited to this new job. I'm forced to face up to my limitations. Which isn't pretty.

Making decisions is a big one. It's not easy to admit, but now that I'm in the hot seat, commanding the enterprise, I find I'm no Captain Kirk.

Instead, I'm being exposed as a bit of a ditherer. And when I go the other way, against my natural disposition, I'm guilty of being rather too rash. A bridge-burner.

Easily offended, defensive and somewhat spiky in my dealings with people.

I can feel myself becoming every useless boss I've ever had. I no longer produce anything of intrinsic value. I could so easily be airbrushed out of the picture. No-one would notice. And I'd have nothing to keep me from slipping back into that dark corridor I've just left behind.

I have to fill my time with something altogether more fulfilling. First day of the rest of my life. It has to be. For my own good.

I think again. I re-examine my position. Take stock. Re-evaluate.

I'm in charge. They have to do what I say. Daunting at first, but then I think 'what would Arturo do?' and eventually the possibilities become clear.

18: CHOCOLATE CAKE

My team is suffering from low morale.

In fact, all these cunts ever seem to do is moan about how no one takes them seriously or bothers to listen to them.

Which is true, but what do they expect? They have absolutely nothing to say.

Joe and Dave, our IT duo look as if the only female they've ever had came delivered in plain brown wrapping paper. And even then they'd probably spend more quality time with the instruction manual.

And then I have Stefan and Martin, our two design gurus, both devotees of postmodern cool. Aloof. Ironic. Disdainful. Grazing on culture like a pair of pure-bred sheep.

But take away the ill-advised haircuts, the geezer-boy

accents, the Star Wars toys and the Lara Croft figurines that litter their desks, and all you have left is that unfortunate kid who got picked on at school for being too fat, too skinny or because he couldn't afford brand name trainers.

And finally there is Sammie. Our boyish assistant. Tall and skinny, yet to fill out, in a cheap static-electricity suit and clumpy slip-on shoes. Pale skin, blood thin lips but mostly silent and unseen. The one who causes me least trouble.

And it's my job to raise their self-esteem.

My only frame of reference is Quentin and his well-meaning attempts to boost moral.

'If you are not part of the solution, you're part of problem.' If I try hard enough I can almost hear his voice reciting his mantra.

I try to think how I can apply this thinking to my new situation.

The problem. The person who is not a team player. The disruptive influence. The one who can't take things seriously. Who won't join in. Refuses to take part. The boat-rocker.

How can you argue with logic like that? Either do as I say without question or be singled out as the problem.

God, that sort of shit used to drive me up the wall, but now that I'm a team leader, in a position of great trust and responsibility, I can, for the very first time, see the potential upside.

I even seem to be picking up the lingo.

And I can see that it will be essential to weed out any individual who won't go along with the group, even if the group is being led up the garden path.

With Arturo as my spirit guide I start to see for the first

time that the peculiar ways in which we are expected to behave in the corporate environment lend themselves rather well to the ridiculous. And it's no great leap to move from the well intentioned to the purely mischievous.

I can think of plenty of examples of awful group exercises that I've had to endure, where we've all resentfully gone along with whatever misguided activity we've been asked to perform. Only in my case, it won't be misguided. But who, honestly, will be able to tell the difference?

I remember one trip to rural Ireland particularly well. If I can top that, I'll have done particularly well. Quentin's idea of a team-building weekend. All of us forced to wear corporate fleeces and brightly-coloured baseball caps at all times. Quentin yelping like an exuberant puppy, asking us over and over to guess what he had in store for us.

A predictable schedule of orienteering, mountain biking and an army-style assault course in the driving rain. Encouraged to work together to solve mental and physical challenges, shouting half-hearted Americanisms to gee each other along.

I remember sniffling and sneezing and stumbling in the leafy mud as the day just refused to come to an end, until Rhys vomited decisively through a combination of cold and fear as he stood shivering and unwilling at the top of a rope slide. Gemma, already close to tears, tipped over the edge into hysterical screaming as the oily yellow liquid showered down onto our upturned faces.

And then that evening, despite the mutinous feelings within the group, we agreed again to be split into two teams with instructions to go forth into the unsuspecting village. Imposing our self-absorbed games upon the hostile locals.

With typical breezy insensitivity, we were told to find out the price of a Guinness from three local pubs, have our picture taken with the Irish flag, sing and learn a shanty and other such ill-advised nonsense. Play was abandoned when the thick-fingered, dark-eyed men in one craggy little pub, unhappy at the big city interruption on their turf, started singing IRA anthems with gusto and menace. About face and a swift return to the hotel, where Quentin quickly retired to his room, only attempting to gloss over events with a shaky smile the next day on the way to the airport.

In the past, my knee-jerk reaction would have been to reject all that team-bonding stuff as forced and synthetic and a particularly cruel and unusual waste of time.

But that was the thinking of the dispossessed, when I was a non-stakeholder. From this side of the fence, I can, for the very first time, see the point of forcing people to do completely pointless things.

The only person who doesn't have to take part is the one in charge. All I have to do is look sage, observe and try not to laugh.

The first thing I do, is give them a common enemy to unite against. It has to be Sammie. The only one who doesn't really deserve it, but also the only one in no position to argue.

After leading by example, I positively encourage the others to pick fault with him whenever the possibility occurs. Not surprisingly, they take to it like naturals.

I give them a week or so to act out and then, as soon as I grow tired of this game, I rein them in.

All this disunity and bickering. I can't be seen to allow that to fester. We can't have a blame culture. Bullying will be severely reprimanded. This team has deep-rooted problems.

What we need here, are some bonding exercises of our own.

When I first set them loose on the grey streets of Holborn armed with a recipe for chocolate cake and no money, I fully expected them to come back empty-handed, annoyed and disheartened.

For my part, I had already mentally rehearsed a series of infuriating responses to their complaints that this was an impossible and quite unreasonable task.

Step 1 – Send them back out the first time they return having admonished them for failing to get into the spirit of the challenge.

Step 2 - Once I had pushed them far enough, I'd hit them with something mindless like:

'The important thing is that you tried. And that you tried as a team. The cake was just a symbol. A way to get you to gel.'

'If you used your initiative to tackle the problem together, then that's the real icing on my cake. That's what's really important. If you learned to work together then we have not wasted our time. And you know what they say about having your cake and not being able to eat it.'

Step 3 – And to finish, single out the slimiest, most earnest head-nodding, ass-kisser of the bunch for singular praise, in order to heighten resentment among the rest of the group.

But just as I was beginning to miss them, impatient for the chance to recite my carefully planned provocation, they return, triumphant. Laughing and joking as one.

Arms round Sammie. Offering me a thick slice of home-made chocolate cake.

19: BUTTERFLY

I'm not sure what's happened, but the transformation in my team is extraordinary.

Ever since I started setting them these ridiculous and frankly, often quite humiliating tasks, they have revealed hidden depths of resource and character.

And they suddenly seem to be enjoying themselves more. Gone are the moping, sullen, uncommunicative misfits that I started with.

Instead, they are now quick to engage. They look people in the eye when talking to them. Walk with a pep in their step, greeting incredulous co-workers on a first name basis with the air of at least an equal, having forgotten or no longer caring that they are merely servelings in the bigger scheme of things.

Sammie has been the biggest revelation. None can bully him now. He just isn't the type to suffer in silence anymore.

It turns out that when you give him something more challenging to do than make tea, run errands or catch the last post, Sammie is like the irresistible force; he simply will not take 'no' for an answer.

He took charge for the very first time on the chocolate cake expedition, taking it upon himself to complete the task when all those around him suddenly had very little to say.

He even went so far as knocking on people's doors with his story of the team's predicament. Explaining the nature of the challenge, appealing to a sense of camaraderie and good sportsmanship.

Playing on the fact that most people simply don't like to say no, until someone finally said 'yes', eager to join in, to share the experience and break their own monotony.

I am puzzled at this new development, but fascinated, almost obsessed by the potential they have shown.

I can only think that they need an excuse to perform. Perhaps like me they have no idea what they like or dislike and perhaps they have no real motivations of their own.

By giving them a challenge, I seem to have wound them up and pointed them in a random direction dictated by my whim. The result has been the complete opposite of what I had planned.

By making it a communal or shared exercise, they have not turned against each other or fallen out as I had wished; instead they've come out of themselves to perform in a way that far exceeds my expectations.

I'm not sure what's at work here. Surely, it can't simply be that they don't want to let each other down or fall short in front of their peers.

No, I'm guessing it's something else. It's more like every lonely individual person in my team has suddenly been gifted the weight of authority that comes from belonging to a group.

It's difficult to grasp but I'm reminded of the daily annoyance of being approached in the street by people that I don't know but who are emboldened by the fact that they represent some charity, company or other organisation.

Or I consider how I behave myself when I cold-call a stranger: 'Hi my name's Khaled, I'm calling from…'

The group, whatever it may be, validates us, giving us an excuse to perform. For my team it seems to have granted them immunity from the normal rules of engagement and allowed them to do the things that they have only ever seen other people do. What's really striking is the fact that this immunity has little or nothing to do with the activities I have them engaged in, which so far have been pretty silly.

And it really has bound them together as an effective unit. I'm initially sickened at the thought, but gradually I come to realise that there is something fascinating and quite powerful at work.

It's an odd feeling but I have to admit that I'm interested again. Perhaps even hooked.

Especially by Sammie.

I still find it hard to believe that he was able to step up when those noisy people around him who make it their business to shout their opinions and inflate their self worth, suddenly had very little to say.

He is still the quietest of the bunch, but the rest treat him with a new-found respect. I want to find out more and see him in action.

20: SOLDIER OF FORTUNE

As the weeks pass, I find that we are actually getting quite busy. My newly invigorated team are starting to prove their worth. Tom and Quentin have referred some work our way. Low-level and intermittent at first, but increasing in volume and value as we gain their respect.

As our reputation grows within the company, other partners and practice heads have sought us out. My time is increasingly spent in meetings. We have been allowed to pitch to clients in person which would have been unthinkable a few short weeks ago, and have been surprisingly slick. First a glossy brochure for a client, then a website, and then some kind of relationship management tool that I can't really pretend to understand.

But I'm only the front man. It's my job to look good in a suit and be smooth and charming. I go to a fair few lunches, exchange a lot of cards, shake many hands. And then, when the confidence is won, I hand over to the people who'll actually do the work.

We're becoming quite the success story. I give a presentation to the rest of the company at Dennis' request. First thing Monday morning of course, before the day starts, only with him that means 7.30 and attendance is more or less compulsory.

It's clear that he feels that his brilliant hand should be seen orchestrating recent developments. I can feel the resentment in the bleary-eyed faces of my audience, as I launch into my spiel with a dry mouth and dull thudding headache.

When I quickly draw to a close, there are some

predictable questions, most of them clearly designed to show the team up as a flash in the pan and me as a loudmouthed upstart who doesn't respect the hierarchy. But instead of blundering through the answers myself, I call Sammie up to answer. Most people won't even know who he is, and will interpret my actions as an obscure but deliberate ploy to slight them in front of Dennis.

I think the most shocked person is red-faced Stefan, who is clearly unhappy at being overlooked by Dennis and sees himself now as leader in waiting. As he has grown more confident in recent weeks, he makes less and less effort to hide the fact that he takes every opportunity to brief against me whenever he comes into contact with a partner. It's something I will have to deal with, as I'm sure that his scheming will find an especially receptive audience now that the light of Dennis Squatter is shining on me once more.

But right now I'm more interested in Sammie. He is unprepared for the question, and has never before been asked to speak in front of so many. I am ready for him to wilt under the incredulous gaze of the partners, but he is unphased, answering the questions clearly and with assurance, if a little quietly. Only Stefan, who continually interrupts from the wings, prevents our team from appearing confident and well-schooled, but even that is a minor annoyance as Dennis asks him to be quiet and attend instead to the laptop/projector to illustrate one of Sammie's answers.

As the meeting breaks Dennis leads an unnecessary and unwelcome round of applause before further marking me out by leading me to his office with an arm round my shoulders.

As I turn to look back over my shoulder, I can see that Sammie has not slipped quietly away. Instead he is helping Stefan pack away the projection kit, saying something to him that takes the baleful look from his face.

Now that we are so much busier, my own personal project has had to be put back. I can no longer afford to send the entire team out on a fool's errand on company time. And I'm running out of ideas.

Since the chocolate cake episode, I sent the team out onto the streets once again to see who could find out the most amount of personal information from the greatest number of complete strangers in an hour, which I billed as test of interpersonal skills. Sammie responded by buying a clipboard for each of the team with instructions to 'interview people' as pollsters.

Then, emboldened by Arturo's more public work, I decide to make a more visible statement. Under the guise of developing their sense of togetherness, I devise a strict uniform for my team to adhere to. I allow for absolutely no customisation or personalisation.

I have them wear plain black trousers, white shirt, buttoned up to the collar with no tie, an identical red badge on four of the five, green for the fifth, all pinned accurately above the left nipple. Their strange look is completed by asking them all to slick down their hair and part it left to right, which obviously annoys Stefan no end as his current hairstyle is a razor-cut mullet with contrasting highlights.

I then ask all four of them to do everything together for an entire week; so if one goes to the toilet they all go to the toilet. The same for meetings, lunch and fag breaks. The man with the green button leads the group, the rest have to follow, and I of course make sure everyone gets a go at the green apart from Stefan, who forfeits his chance early on by teasing up his hair ever so slightly as I knew he would.

The five of them obviously caused quite a stir at the office but I refuse them permission to explain themselves. So after the initial surprise and questions they have to endure rather a lot of mickey-taking, some anger and hostility and a fair amount of apprehension, as the rumour spreads that this is another one of Dennis' pilot schemes, which could soon be rolled out across the company.

To my surprise, being marked out as so obviously different and apart from the rest of their group does actually seem to help with their togetherness and not simply in terms of developing a siege mentality. Once again Sammie, who is the least aggravated and embarrassed of the team, meets the challenge with gusto. He uses his leadership period to instil a bit of play and humour, getting the rest to learn routines for walking in step back and forth from the loo, or simultaneously pulling out from their desks and swivelling their chairs before getting crisply to their feet on his command. Even I have to smile.

But in future I'll have to be a bit more careful; this latest stunt in the office has ruffled quite a few feathers. On the second day, I'm called into Dennis' office and asked to explain my team's bizarre behaviour. I tell him that I've recently read a radical article in Soldier of Fortune, which discussed tried and tested military techniques for breaking in troops and developing discipline and esprit de corps within the ranks.

I then thank him for creating an environment that encourages fresh thinking and initiative amongst his lieutenants. I tell him I've already seen a marked change in my team and that I'll write him up a full report at the end of the week. He asks me for a copy of the article, telling me to keep up the good work, but to make allowances for 'entrenched thinking in certain quarters'. I just about managed not to salute before leaving his room.

Even so, I've kept things pretty quiet after Soldier of Fortune week, and despite being busy and doing relatively well, I can feel the boredom returning. Whatever I think up next will have to be off-site and out of hours.

21: CASANOVA

They say that the average man thinks about sex every six minutes or so. They say that one in three people have office affairs. They say if you see somebody everyday, you will begin to look at them in a different way.

Gemma is obvious. She's young. She's pretty. She's newly blonde and glossy. And she has become increasingly aware of how she can trade on all of this.

All the characteristics that I say I find entirely unattractive. I've convinced myself that I want an alternative brand; one that is more discerning and marks me out as a sophisticated consumer.

But now that I'm not sitting opposite her, I find myself making excuses to walk past her desk, or to go see Tom, which allows me to sneak sideways glances at her. I don't like the idea of being attracted to her, but I'm unable to deny it.

The thing to do is not to let it show. That would be humiliating. She wouldn't want me and I'd be rejected. But what I find worse than that is the prospect of making any kind of public admission of attraction in front of the group.

But I know that I really do like her, I always have. I liked the sweet shy girl with the awkward smile that first joined the company. And I would often find myself saying things or acting in a demonstrative manner for her benefit. But I'd never say anything to her directly. I'd ignore her. I always do. I'd like to think it's a tactic, but it's not really even a choice. I can only talk to women or show an interest when there is no one else around, or when I'm anonymous in a crowd of drunken strangers, and even then it's not easy.

I'm awkward, confrontational, and come across as having something to prove. Even when all I have to do is nod my head and smile into some eager shining eyes to guarantee a sale, I find myself more often than not saying something extreme or acting in some weird, bizarre way that is guaranteed to blow the deal. I often find myself telling one of my lies, but never one that paints me as more attractive.

The problem is the girls I want don't want me and I can't ignore the faults I see in the ones that do. This rule can even apply within the same person.

There was one night with Gemma, not that long ago,

where we came close. Actually I'm not all that sure, because I can never really tell, but I know something definitely happened between us. It was at the company Christmas party, which already sounds cheap and tawdry.

But it was a function so the girls wore off-the-shoulder gowns and strappy shoes and the men wore dinner jackets. For some reason we were all supposed to wear wigs, because we're the kind of company where you don't have to be crazy to work, but it helps. So while my male co-workers donned Elvis sideburns or nylon afros, the girls went sleek and sexy. I, of course, refused to take part and only conceded to dying my hair dark blue, because 'hey I'm different'.

I was surprised throughout the night to find myself receiving quite a bit of female attention, most of it of a playful kind, which again left me feeling suspicious and out of sorts, as if an elaborate practical joke was being played out at my expense. But I eventually relaxed and I have to admit I quite enjoyed playing bashful and awkward to the teasing and felt secretly pleased to be dragged reluctantly on to the dancefloor.

And all the time I could see Gemma in her group, far away from me. Looking unusually fresh and natural in a simple black dress and a dark bobbish wig that changed the entire complexion of her face and neck and shoulders.

As for myself, I felt happy, and at one with the people around me, so when she turned and caught my eye, I didn't look away, but smiled instead. A warm and easy smile that felt so natural for me to give away. It really was ever so strange, the sensation of feeling so open and calm, actually comfortable in my own skin.

And later, when I was laughing and dancing and enjoying the company of those who were so generous to me, I felt a tap on the shoulder, and I saw Gemma again. Half-smiling, mouth closed, eyes tilted up at me. Sexy, so sexy mischief in her voice as she spoke, asking me why I hadn't asked her to dance yet.

And for once I didn't feel the gaze of all the people who might know my desire, and did not react rashly to the coquettish nature of the game in which she asked me to join her. I said nothing, but took her by the hand, and for one moment everything was perfect. I liked her, she liked me and we danced.

And then when the moment ended, she stepped away and smiled again. I saw in her face a secret look. She wasn't a naïve, young girl, or a weary career woman, or anything I'd ever seen in her before. She showed me a glimpse of someone else waiting to be discovered. And then she walked away, to the other side of the room, leaving an invitation to me, half hanging in the air.

We'd said very little, and I think that I know, or guess but I'm unsure, that she wanted me to make the next move in the ritual, to have me say or do something in return for her having approached me first. Well that's how it felt, and I think that's how it's usually done. Had I gone over without thinking, I think that's how it might even have worked out.

But I just couldn't be sure. A slow paralysis of indecision started to sour my mood. The longer I waited, the more unreal the moment between us seemed, until I convinced myself that it was nothing. The confidence and certainty drained from my person and into the bottom of the glass that I kept emptying again and again.

So finally, somehow I convinced myself that her intentions were purely malicious, and that she was flirting intentionally to taunt me, trying to provoke me into stepping over the line, so I'd make a pass at her that she could publicly refuse.

I somehow knew she'd hurt and humiliate me and have one over me for forever more.

I don't know quite how I did it, but I externalised my insecurity and channelled it into impotent anger at the very same girl that I desired for so long and who had lifted me, briefly, so high.

And so finally at the end of the night, when she was ready to leave and came to me once more, asking me where I had gone, I cut her dead, rude and vicious, in front of a group of our peers, and things have become steadily worse between us ever since.

22: HARDCORE

I'm not very good with women. And I can't play football. And I know that when there is violence in the air, my heart beats funny and I cower away apologetic, shitted up and bottled out.

I'm tall and strong and not bad looking at all, but when it comes to all the crucial tests of testosterone and competition, I'm not much of a man at all.

Which is alright most of the time because we don't live in the jungle. Or on the Serengeti plains.

But tonight is one of those nights when those bare and elemental truths may well smack me in the face. And kick me in the head. And stamp on my useless balls.

In an effort to learn more about him, and also to annoy Stefan, I let Sammie choose the location of a team night out. And I told him to keep it authentic and spare us nothing.

I said that in order to 'bond' we must 'know' and 'understand' 'each other'. And in order to 'know' and 'understand' we must 'walk a mile in each other's shoes'. Not literally of course. But we must observe each other in our 'natural environment' to see how we each 'tick'.

I can't be certain that anyone bought this line. And I'm certain that Sammie didn't. I see a growing spark of recognition in his eyes everyday.

But it is of absolutely no consequence, because they have to do as I say. The old 'you're either with me or against me' has robbed them of their right to reply.

Only this time I wish one of them had objected. It turns out that quiet, pale Sammie who says so little at work is an MC out of hours, for whom words are precious and not to be given away.

And under duress he's taken us on sightseeing tour of his secret world. First there is the rave in a dingy sweaty room on the outskirts of London.

We arrive in convoy in aggressive cars with aggressive drivers. Sovereign rings, bad teeth and yellow skin up close. Sammie's crew up close. Laughing, shouting, chewing, spitting. Hyenas. Up close.

Sammie quiet at first. Uncomfortable. With me and Martin and Joe and Stefan in tow. All of us nervous. Unsure how to behave.

But then he takes to the stage, backed by a DJ and a crowd of hyped up extras that have travelled along with him.

Machine gun patter. Microphone distortion. Sparse

concrete beats and solid sine-wave bass. An unfeeling grimy noise. And Sammie riding it all, inciting the crowd, with nursery rhyme flow.

I can't understand a word he says but it has a rhythm and aggression to make the heart beat faster. The air is thick with the smell of powerful cross-bred hydro-ponic weed. I see mixed-race teens with cloaked faces popping pills and snorting powder from their fists. But this isn't a love-in or even a shared experience. There are no smiles at strangers or back rubs or talking pleasant nonsense. It's everyone behind their own grill, with their own menace.

This is the sound and feel and smell of technology.

After the show we do not stay to party. Sammie and his boys corner the promoter and demand money immediately. The promoter shucks and jives, and promises to come back to them later, but Sammie gets right up in his face, and demands the money now.

I can't remember the words. A secret dialect spoken in estates and street corners outside off-licences and convenience stores in every town by acrylic kids that we look to avoid. But the threat is clear to everyone.

The untidiness of violence is seconds away. The black-jacketed men who let us pass at the door circle close. It calls for a moment of calm. This is the last thing I want to be caught up in. I want to plead with Sammie to be reasonable and sensible and civilised. I want him to back away and let us all leave quietly.

'Pussy.' If I speak up now I know that's what they'll call me. 'Cunt.' I know that's what they'll say. 'Wanker.'

But I like pussy. I like cunt. I like to wank. I like them all so much better than a bottle in the face. This is ridiculous. I want to negotiate. Reach a compromise.

Somehow I manage to keep my mouth shut and watch as the promoter tries to turn away. I watch in soundless horror as Sammie puts his hands on him. Spins him around. The crowd instinctively pulls back. The bouncers step forwards and I'm frozen to the spot.

'Don't walk away from me you cunt. I want my money. Now.'

Sammie's face is inches away from the promoter, spraying him with spit. He is flanked by his crew. More figures step forwards from the dance floor.

At first I think they are backing up the promoter and I want to cry, but they step in behind Sammie, who I can now see is rolling deep in this club.

Although he is shouting to be heard above the roar of the club, Sammie is calm.

The bouncers back off. The promoter forces a smile. He shows open palms. He is conciliatory. He wants to calm things down. He hands Sammie a roll of tens.

Game over. Sammie wins.

Later that night, when we have driven back into the heart of town, and navigated our way through a dark estate to a devastated flat high above the city, I look at Sammie again.

He is conducting a radio show. On a pirate station. The room looks long abandoned as a home. Cheap, mismatched furniture, no carpet. Writing and spray-paint on the walls. Gerry-rigged sound and broadcasting equipment. And in the corner the flashing lights of a fruit machine, standing ignored against the wall.

The room is full of hooded figures, who keep coming in and leaving. Nine or ten people present at any one time. There are rituals and greetings. Grunts and nods.

I keep quiet and observe. Sammie hands me several mobiles and puts me in charge of taking shout-outs and dedications from the listeners. Both to give me something to do and to break the ice for me with the people in the room, who all take great amusement at the way I answer and speak on the phone.

I can see that Sammie is completely at ease. I can see that he is so much more than the person at work. He commands respect both through his standing and his actions.

This is a world that he has helped to create.

I think how much more I could do. How I could create a world of my own. How Sammie could be so useful.

23: RANDOM SHIFT

So the change in my team is plain for all to see: they have gone from invisible to hard to ignore. But there has also been a change in me. One that is less obvious.

Unlike Sammie and the rest, I've always looked and sounded the part; I've been able to fake and bluster my way through. But it is a brittle bluff that runs only surface deep. Scrape away the veneer and you find a man without belief. Worse still a man without focus.

I would say I have this idea about what makes us human. A recurring theme. I would say it is the ability to doubt. To feel insecure. The difference between man and machine. Man and animal. But then the sting in the tail: it is almost always true that the most remarkable humans, the ones that we allow to ascend, are those that seem only to have all-consuming belief. Allowing them to act without hesitation, or crippling knowledge of their limitations. Performing like machines, shedding that which I say makes them human.

The field of achievement has no relevance, although some we celebrate over others. Sports over politics. Wealth over religion. Celebrity over all.

And what makes the freedom fighter and the terrorist the same is belief. Blinkered conviction. Total belief unfettered by thought or indecision.

Which even now makes me think of random shift. On your iPod or CD player. Sure, we can understand that. But how about all around us, in life. Throwing up tricky combinations and unexpected discoveries like Sammie and perhaps even this power of The Group that I'm struggling to understand.

What makes one man celebrated and the next despised is also surely random shift. Well that's what I'd argue.

All of which sounds great at five in the morning, round a middle class dinner table.

And so you keep on talking and it all makes sense. You use random shift as a means to compare the child molester to the foster mother. They are all driven to do what they do. They act without being crippled by choice. People laugh and you even pause for a second yourself, dazzled by the icy clarity of your own thinking.

And in the morning or the next day you half-realise

that you are the one wearing blinkers. It's only by numbing yourself that you have any belief in what you say. The rest of the time you know you're not true. You don't even have any concept of true.

I realise that I am, or at least I was, a cosseted conscientious objector. From the whole thing. I didn't want to get involved. No sense of purpose, no beliefs, no love. Holding the world at arm's length; refusing to engage.

So there it is: while half the world is starving and speaks in their own tongue, my powdery, English-speaking thoughts only seem to work as an avoidance tactic. An elaborate way to opt out.

Or so it used to be. I now sense something else. Things are coming together and there is a subtle shift. A hardening of intention. I am less inhibited by the debilitating thought patterns of old and instead feel the need to act and act soon. I don't know what I am to do but I no longer doubt that something will happen.

All it will take is a little random shift.

I spoke to my father today. A familiar pattern to the conversation. I feel I am trying to trap an elusive animal:

'Hi Dad, how are you?'

'Khaled?' he always sounds surprised to hear from me, as if I've been away or even missing for a very long time.

'Yes Dad it's me. How are you?'

'Everything is fine. How is your work?'

'Fine, Dad, fine, you know the same old thing. How is everyone?'

'Fine.'

'Any news Dad? Anything happening?'

'No everything is the same as always.'

'And you're well?'

'Yes, my health is good.'

'You know Dad, I'm thinking of changing my job. Doing something completely different. What do you think?'

'You know best.'

'You know Dad, it could be a bit of a risk, maybe leave here and do something for myself. What do you think? Do you think it might be a good idea or not?'

'It's up to you Khaled. You know what you are doing.'

'Yeah, well maybe. I just want to hear what you think.'

'You always make up your own mind Khaled, so what is there for me to say?'

'Ok Dad. Speak soon.'

'Ok bye.'

24: SMART BOMB

Email to Philip Mould, Torrid Media:

Philip,

How are things? Quentin asked me to drop you a line. As you know he's away for the next fortnight, but Tom will cover day-to-day account handling as usual.

As the new head of Silverback's multimedia team, I've been asked to explore any areas of mutual benefit that may exist between us. We have access to an impressive client list and you of course have great online expertise which combined could have the makings of potentially great fit.

You'll remember me as Quentin's copywriter — the last thing I did for you was that Cruzin piece, about your relationship with PMC — how did that work out for you?

Anyway how is next week looking for you? I can come to you. Let me know if you have time for an initial meeting.

Best wishes
Khaled

Reply email from Philip Mould:

Khaled,
Great to hear from you, bro. Congratulations on the promotion - in charge of the multimedia team — sounds v. interesting. Really loved the Cruzin piece, as did PMC — glad that we haven't lost you.
Love to hook up — how about Thursday pm, last thing in the day, we'll meet at my office and we can chat over a meal.
How's that sound?

As a courtesy, I forward Philip's email to Tom – minus the first line.

Later that afternoon, he finds his way to my desk. He seems a little wary and is uncomfortable with the idea that Philip has contacted me directly. He is harassed and short of time with Quentin away, but he insists that if I'm meeting Philip, he's coming too.

I agree and act as if I'd like nothing better than to get out of it. I tell Tom to leave it with me.

I'm relying on the fact that Tom will be too busy to chase me up, and that if I leave it the last minute to remind him, he won't be able to tag along.

A little risky perhaps, but I've no doubt it'll work.

A first step. To what I'm not sure, but I am possessed with a new sense of purpose. I have this strong instinct that the all the little details will simply fall into place.

25: HELLO, IS IT ME YOU'RE LOOKING FOR?

I've been to Torrid's offices before. Shoreditch. Warehouse. Brown exposed brick. Pastel computers. Pasty faces.

I am kept waiting the obligatory fifteen minutes in the loosely defined holding area. I pick up a trade magazine and use it to mask the fact that I'm glancing up every few seconds to check out the icy receptionist. She's a face-painted uber-blonde, who ignores me with a well-practised air.

Anna, Philip's PA, eventually bustles through and leads me inside. She speaks to me in a tone and pitch that makes me wonder if she has mistaken me for a small, deaf and perhaps slightly backwards child.

I expose my teeth and bob my head in response. She appears to appreciate the fact that I have not attempted to engage her in any conversation and seems satisfied by the unintelligible noises that I expel from the very back of my throat.

Philip is predictably in mid-conversation on the phone but motions for me to sit as Anna melts away. His office is small but extraordinarily busy. Leafy potted plants, black leather, framed awards, sharp metallic angles, and a shiny espresso machine all compete for attention as he glowers across his ugly perspex desk.

I use the moment to study my opponent.

Philip is an incredibly short, hairy, intense fist of a man. His dial is as always set at 11. He rolls his eyes at me to indicate his opinion of whoever he is speaking to and continues to bellow into the phone.

I remain calm and stare evenly back, unmoved by his little play. In my mind I have him talking to his mother. And she is telling him to wrap up warm if he's going out and not to be back late because he needs his sleep.

He winds down his call and immediately reaches for a remote, which he points, like a pistol, just past my head. I see that his fingers are short and stubby, but his nails are long and sharp and fabulously manicured.

The air in the room vibrates to the sound of gangsta bass. A Tonka-toy criminal drops crude Walter Mitty fantasies with little wit or poetry.

Philip is trying to shock and impress me in equal measure with this juvenile territorial display, but I'm also playing a game – I've decided that I won't be the one to speak first.

I settle back comfortably in my seat. Philip swivels around in his, doing the white man shuffle.

The track finally fades, there is silence. Ten seconds, twenty. Philip stares at me. I stare at him, a small smile on my lips. Philip cracks first.

'So, I don't know about you, but I want to get wasted tonight.'

The last ditch throw of a desperate man.

Now creative or media types don't usually go for Blush, a 'gentleman's' club, with more than a hint of dirty money but Philip is old school, he's all about the money, the dirtier the better.

A massive ego offensive to impress, greetings from big men, tricky hand-shakes, big demonstrative gestures, shoulders pounded, ropes lifted, curtains parted, private rooms. Big bottles of champagne, tiny dresses, a mix of East End and eastern European accents.

But I'm unmoved. I feel like I'm travelling through a tunnel. Sound is distant, muted, colours washed out. A trance of calm and tranquillity. Stillness. An unfamiliar state but I am completely comfortable. At ease with myself. Focused. In control.

The less I react, the more Philip lays it on. Thick. And fast. A full frontal assault. Crass and dumb. A parody of himself. So much undirected energy. I recognise him as one of my own. Lost. In pain. Desperate for approval. Hungry. Searching for something.

He keeps on building. Louder. Faster. Maniacal. Wanting me to join him. Offering me everything that he knows. Champagne. Cigars. Girls. Whiskey. And cocaine.

Expensive, creamy, high-grade cocaine. All the riches he has to give. But nothing for me. I have no desire that he can fulfil. He is weak and confused. Unused to commanding so little response. I'm here to help him. The crescendo comes and goes.

And then, when I sense the time is right, I make my pitch to Philip. The fact that I have spoken very little gives my words weight. His face is contorted into a toothy scowl, and his stubby fingers twist and pull at the wire-wool hair on the backs of his hands.

I notice it all but filter it out. I speak with a sense of purpose, although I am unaware of what I will say. The words flow easily like the barren lies I once used to tell. But there is some other force that drives me now.

The tight contours of Philip's face give way to a smooth, serene expression. His shoulders drop, and his hands become still as the tension leaves his body. He seems to sink into the warm, rich brown leather of his chair as he listens quietly to what I have to say. My tone is soft and gentle. Washing over him. Soothing him. And although it is nothing like he imagined it would be, I know that he has finally experienced a moment that feels rich and intense.

I have him now and we both know it. I leave before the spell is broken. The girls who have been hovering in the middle distance suddenly descend, but Philip is still staring at the spot where I was once sat.

Afterwards I try to remember what I said. The more I focus, the looser I find my recollection of key moments. I am aware of feeling tightly zoned, all distractions greyed out, hardly any peripheral vision.

I can see Philip's face, or at least his eyes, nose and mouth, super-clear in macro-focus and I have a memory of colours, and textures beyond that, muted in the velvety darkness of the room.

All I know for certain is that I told the truth.

I remember saying that what he does is wrong and that he must know this himself.

Nothing confrontational, just a statement of fact. I told him that he is lost. He has success. He has brutishly asserted his will upon others to achieve what he has but he flaunts it.

All his clumsy displays of power and influence tell me that he is desperately clinging on to all that he has accumulated but it is not enough.

And I'm not saying he needs to give it all up, but I tell him that I can clearly see that he is in need of something more.

My memory, which has been warm and foggy, jolts into clear, cold focus as I think of how I left him.

'You are restless. You are looking for something new. Something that consumes you. And is worth doing not because it's a smart move, but because it makes you feel alive.'

'Am I talking about making your mark? Leaving something behind? I don't know. Yet.'

'Be ready, I'll be in touch.'

26: ASAKO

Jun has been out a lot recently seeing a new girl. Her name is Asako, she is 23 and has been in London for just over a year. Tonight he is in the small flat we share, and I meet her for the first time.

She looks like a highly glossed, highly accessorised, miniature pop-princess. With different make-up and another outfit, I will find it hard to recognise her again, such is the overpowering impact of her look.

After the clumsy introductions, we settle into an uneasy awkwardness. They would clearly rather be alone, and while Jun prepares a meal for the two of them, I am vaguely angered at the thought of feeling like trespasser in my own home.

I cannot avoid the idea that Asako has taken an instant dislike to me and that Jun is embarrassed by me. I start to convince myself that she may be a little racist. The Japanese often are.

But I know these feelings well. They come from fear and they no longer overwhelm. They are now the return of an old obsolete friend who can only remind me of who I used to be.

With some effort, I engage the two of them in conversation.

I discover that Asako has ambitions to be an idol. In a band or by herself. She doesn't care. She has an interest in the look and the lifestyle but not really the material.

She has entered numerous shows at home in Japan and also here in the UK, but she has never auditioned for a band.

I am attracted by the thinness of her dream. To be on

stage, to be on TV, to be photographed and seen is all. It is perfect, uncomplicated and pure. And so wonderfully common.

27: OPINIONS AND ARSEHOLES

My first ad reads:

NEW FACES WANTED
Do you have a dream? Should you be seen? Should we be paying attention to you? Don't settle for ordinary – go for what you deserve.
Send name, contact and photo to The Group, PO Box 1611, CRO 1WW. CVs will not be considered.

It's a tiny ad and deliberately vague that runs in *The Stage* and the classified section of *Time Out*. Philip mails it to various agents and other contacts in the industry without question.

I am staggered by the response. I have hundreds of applications. Only about half follow the rules of sending a photo only. The rest strive to be different and worthy of special attention and send all manner of things to convince me.

There are showreels, demo tapes, pieces of writing, ranging from 'all about me', to drama, poetry and comedy.

Artworks that range from the polished to the disturbed. Several people hit upon the same idea of sending no photo at all as if to tease me into picking them.

Then there are random objects sent – a desk toy with somebody's name, where there'd usually be a corporate logo. Flowers. Chocolates. Carefully packaged drugs. A lot of cuddly toys. Some disfigured.

A witty and well-observed home-made calendar, featuring a young woman in a parody of Pirelli poses against a series of miserable suburban backdrops.

Another sends a mobile phone in the belief that I will be bowled over by the initiative he has shown that allows him to call me direct.

Another simply features the word 'please' printed repeatedly on a ten foot long roll of paper, that ends with the phrase 'pick me'.

It all seems borderline psychotic, but these people are hungry and shouting to be heard. One even sends a visual of a brain scan, which not only seems pretentious but also desperately wide of the mark.

The pictures are no better. Ranging from the soft-focus, smile up at the camera, portfolio shots, to snaps of people on holiday, or with friends, having fun, drinking, dancing. Some are in fancy dress, others in drag. Pick me. Pick me.

Then there are those young men and some women who scowl at the camera, convinced of their own youth, truth and beauty.

There are also the inevitable erotic poses. Pictures of body-parts some featuring a face, others not. Middle-aged women in leather-look plastic and imitation lace. Tawdry bustiers, thongs and slips. Red lips frozen open to reveal the fleshy tongue within. Bare-chested old men with oil glistening on their sallow skin. Whips, ropes, chains and cuffs. Flashers, nudists, exhibitionists and other less easily labelled hobbyists.

A surprising number of people send pictures of animals; others send pictures of celebrities. These I find most puzzling of all.

There are men and women of all ages. From all backgrounds. Different colours and races. So many names. So many hopes. Bright-eyed. All dreaming of the same thing. To defy the odds, to be singled out, recognised. One out of so many, competing for the same prize.

After some deliberation, I cannot decide whether to keep the ones that have stuck to the rules or the ones that have gone that extra mile.

I throw them all away instead.

Random shift, baby. Random Shift.

28: PHILIP MOULD

Philip is a man of action. He cannot wait for instruction. He calls me. He is in a highly agitated state. He needs to start.

I match him with Sammie. I bring the two of them together. One newly confident and self-possessed, the other anxious but, as always, hungry to win.

'I want you to work together as a team. Sammie you take the lead, you've done this sort of thing before.'

At this point I have explained nothing to Sammie; not attempted to recruit him in any way, but as I expect he does not waver or question in any way. I suspect he understands more than me.

I can see Philip's eyes bulging at the insult.

'I have something planned, something big. But before we do that I need you to experience first hand the power that you wield.'

'You need to know what it is to lead and be led. Experience the power you feel being part of something bigger than yourself. And then harness that power to lead others.'

Sammie is with me all the way. He has come far and is willing to continue on his path. He stares back openly, without question or fear. His acceptance is so complete, I almost feel tears forming in my eyes.

Philip is more excitable. He needs answers. The need to assess and make decisions is ingrained. The need to have us feel the weight of his personality is far greater.

'So what do you have planned? What is it you want to do? How do I fit in? When do we start?'

'Philip, I have no blueprint. I am uninterested in results. What will be, will be. I just want you to discover what I have discovered; that people wish to be led. And they want to belong. This is the most powerful drive of all. And if they could only dare to be honest, you would see they don't really care about being tricked or deceived. They happily gather wool about their own eyes, so they can ignore the price they pay to belong.'

I sense that Philip is troubled by the notion that he has been led. He shuffles nervously, a bundle of motion, his hands touching his face, his mouth, his hair. Face sweating, mouth dry, licking his lips. I imagine that he

might be high. With Philip it's actually quite hard
to know.

'Philip, have you taken something?'

He is unfazed by the question, happier to be on
familiar ground.

'Just a couple of lines – do you want me rack some
out?'

He looks over at Sammie and then back at me, eager
to do more with us, or by himself if we decline.

'No Philip. Not for me. Or for Sammie. You do what
you like. But I want you to know that the things that
happen and the way you feel when you use are only the
merest glimpse of your true person.'

I can see Philip drifting away, an auto-response to the
lecture he thinks is coming.

'Philip, look at me. I don't disapprove. Taking drugs is
just another sign to me that you want something more. It's
your choice, I just want to show you something else. But I
want you to understand, that what you see and
experience tonight will be no less true because you have
taken your drugs. Don't use them as an excuse and
convince yourself of anything else in the morning.'

I sit in a corner of the room and watch my boys go to
work. We are in the Ship pub again. I choose it
deliberately because I know that Sammie and I will feel
less anonymous here and there are familiar faces from
Silverback who can see and hear everything we do.

Again this presents no obstacle to Sammie. He glides

about the room, with Philip in tow, uncaring that people from the rigid hierarchy of the office are uneasy that they should even be seen together.

I watch them closer and wonder what they'll come up with. At first they approach groups of people. Then they talk to single men. Then women. And then they talk to groups again. I've given them no specific instructions but they understand completely. I marvel at how little it takes. First take one and have him speak to five and in turn have this five each speak to another five. With more direction I see how easy this could all be.

I don't know what they are saying. I don't know what actions they are trying to induce. But I see them clicking into gear. Intent, focused and clear as they gather those around unto them.

Later when I ask Sammie he tells me that Philip told them he was looking for sponsors, people willing to volunteer. Intense and persuasive, he told them that it was up to every single one of us to make a difference. Our duty as citizens.

He told them that he hadn't given up yet but he was close to despair at the apathy of our times. With a rousing passion he set down his declaration and made his call to arms. He told them he had no time for cowardly people who turn a blind eye to what's going on around them. He said he wanted warriors with a social conscience instead, those who are unwilling to sit by and do nothing while all around us our society decays.

Good Samaritans that will give up their time, money and energy to fight the scourge of drugs on our street.

I'm amazed at his sense of humour.

29: NATURAL SELECTION

With the responses to my ad piling up during the day and more missions to test the credulity of our fellow men by night, I barely go into work now.

And when I do turn up, I'm barely there. No one seems to mind, as Sammie has taken over, and it is now accepted he has a direct line to me.

I am home. I stare at my mirrored reflection, wondering whether to shave away the beard that is growing long upon my face.

I have more important work to do.

The number of responses to my ad has been phenomenal. It has run for two weeks but already my flat is full of bags of mail, spilling out all over my bedroom and into the kitchen, in the hall and covering the floor of the living room.

Jun has told me I have to pull the ad. Enough is enough. He doesn't understand, each new response gives me strength and feeds my sense of certainty. But eventually I do cancel it: I have more than enough for what I need.

I need to choose The Group.

I summon Sammie and Philip to the flat. Jun is there, with Asako, who both agree to help, eager to clear away the mess, both of them growing increasingly unsure of my behaviour.

We need to employ science and intuition. Who will we choose?

I ask Asako for her favourite number. She says seven. Lucky seven.

I choose out every seventh bag of post. The rest I dismiss. I feel a wrench as I see Jun and Philip carry out so many bags of comfort from my cocoon.

Sammie and Asako are opening the remaining few bags and arranging the mail alphabetically at my request.

I can feel Asako's interest heighten with every letter and package she opens. A fair number are from people in their teens or early twenties. They are bright and sparkle. She can see herself fitting right in.

She asks if she can read the advert, and eventually asks: 'What is The Group? What is it for?'

To his credit, Sammie doesn't even look up at me, he just continues to sort. My heart swells with pride.

'Asako, there is no group. I made it up. It's nothing.'

'But what for? Why would you do that? What about all these people?'

'It's nothing Asako. It only exists because these people want it to exist.'

'No. It must be true. Why won't you tell me what it is? Why are you doing it?'

'I can't explain Asako. I don't have an answer. Maybe you could call it a trick, or a cheat. Maybe you could see it as a social experiment. I don't know. I just want to see what happens.'

She continues with her work unsatisfied by what I have said, whereas I feel ecstatic. I can picture myself on TV giving the same answers. Enigmatic, composed.

I am gripped, suddenly, by an surge of energy. Overwhelming. Intense. I am truly high for the first time.

I jump to my feet and start to kick over the carefully arranged piles of mail.

Asako shrieks, jumping back, her hands at her mouth. Sammie watches on.

I grab two handfuls of mail and shout:

'What are these? The Es? We could have the next Eminem in here, or the next Tracey Emin. Or Elvis. Waiting to be discovered. All these people, waiting to be discovered. In our hands. I've got the whole world in my hands.'

I am elated, laughing wildly. Screaming.

'Throw them out. Out. Out. What about the Bs. The bloody B'. B for Richard Burton, for Bukowski, Bill and Ben. Chuck 'em out, brother. All of them and the As and the Cs. Easy. Easy E and a brother called Ice Cube. Easy as ABC, keep the Js, Jackson 5, Jackson Sisters. I believe in miracles. Don't you?'

There are tears flowing from my eyes. I am laughing so hard, I almost choke.

'Now find me a really scruffy one, all creased up with stains. And a picture of an ugly one. A real minger. And one with a spelling mistake in the first paragraph. Oh yeah and a handwritten one that's impossible to read. Yeah we'll keep those. Congratulations, you've been selected to go through to our next round.'

I'm dancing round the middle of the room, throwing applications above my head.

'Come on help me choose. Feel the power. It could be you. It could be you. It could be yooooou.'

Asako is edging away, her wide eyes on me, her back against the wall.

Sammie jumps up and shouts, 'Alright, let's have it.

Throw them up in the air. All those that land on the sofa, right way up we keep.'

I hug him, delighted by his genius thought.

Later when Jun and Philip return, it is to a trashed room and a shaken Asako.

Jun is angry and wants to know what I've done.

I am exhausted and feel all used up by my earlier frenzy. But I look up at him from the floor and say evenly.

'I've chosen them. It is done. I have the first fifty.'

'Chosen what? You fucking psycho. What are you up to?'

I am content to let him shout himself out, but I notice both Sammie and Philip are instantly alert and have both tensed up as if readying for physical action. Jun senses the subtle change in the atmosphere of the room and quietens down.

'I've chosen the first fifty. And from those I will choose The Group. And The Group will be nothing at all.'

I feel empty now as I say the words, strangely dislocated almost as if someone else has spoken and I can barely hear him from far, far away.

I am awoken in the early hours by a quiet knock at my bedroom door. I sit up in my bed and the door opens. I see the shape of Asako in the first light of the day, as she steps inside and carefully shuts the door soundlessly behind her. She knows that The Group is nothing. She knows that it is a lie. But she wants to join anyway. I welcome her in.

30: CLAUSTROPHOBIA

Philip is beginning to irritate me. He is unhappy at missing the selection process. Selection for what? This thing is starting to take a life of its own.

I need to step back and make some decisions.

Sammie is holding down the office, but all is not well. Management may not have noticed my absences but they scrutinise figures without mercy.

And the team: they are becoming restless and reverting back to their old sullen ways. They need focus and they need a leader.

I make arrangements to promote Sammie to my number two, giving him a hefty raise. This may prove a little tricky to pass through so to smooth the way I arrange for Philip to award the team some unspecified work — Project: The Group, for which he pays us a large retainer. Sammie is credited for winning the work.

I placate Philip by leaving him charge of contacting the fifty. He insists on having Asako assist him. She is keen to be involved but would rather be one of the chosen. I cannot decide if Philip is trying to fuck her or just needs someone to be in charge of. I'm not entirely sure which of these desires will be greater, or whether they are even mutually exclusive.

Philip is also working on PMC Records to secure us some audition space to greet and whittle down our fifty.

I look again at the fifty applications that we have chosen. We have pictures of about half, and they are not the worst of the bunch: most are youthful and attractive, which I know will help for whatever I come up with. I am beginning to recognise their faces and remember their names and realise that they are people like me for the first time.

Things are coming together. It's all becoming a little too real, a little too fast. I wish I could just run away.

31: THE GOSPEL SINGER

The old church is cold and empty. Noise echoes easily against the stone walls and up into the high ceiling. The yellow light from the stained glass is muted, picking out motes of dust in the air.

Jesus' face is calmly carved in gleaming wood high above. He stares sightlessly down to his side, his face at rest while his body twists against the cross.

Everything is still and I am ready.

There is the sound of footsteps approaching, slow and sure.

Sammie is at my side:

'They are here boss. They are gathering outside.'

I am tempted to take my place at the pulpit, but resist. I shall watch unobserved from the wings. Just in case it all goes wrong.

My invitation says 9.15 sharp. The church fills with the noise of nervous expectation.

We close the doors at 9.25. I count forty-six people. There are three late arrivals, who are told to go home, and one no-show.

I take a seat at the very back of the room, nearest the door that has been closed and bolted shut from the outside by Jun.

The noise level is rising. People notice the unmanned video cameras on tripods in the four corners of the room.

I see two people sit by themselves. Both men. One young and skittish, the other middle-aged and sure. They sit on opposites sides of the room, but both shuffle some way along their pew, taking them away from the central aisle, before they take a seat.

There are three other mixed groups of two or three or four, who take seats nearer the centre of the room and settle into a stilted rhythm of introductions and quiet conversation.

Of those still standing, one young intense man I recognise is ignoring everyone, deliberately walking around the perimeters of the room, inspecting the church, the windows and the cameras. He passes close by me without a glance.

The majority have formed a loose group that ebbs and flows in the centre of the aisle, meeting and greeting. Perfect social animals at an early morning gathering.

The sound of voices and laughter peaks and starts to settle as several minutes pass.

The group in the centre of the aisle starts to fragment as more time passes without any interruption or instruction. More people sit, others disperse to the edges of the room. There are nervous glances, fixed smiles, a shrugging of shoulders.

At 9.45 as rehearsed, Philip enters the church from an anteroom and takes to the altar flanked by Sammie and Asako.

There is a hush. He waits until all faces are staring into his.

'Greetings. Ladies and Gentleman. Welcome to The Group. When I ask you to, could everyone standing please make their way to the front of the church, where they will be greeted by my colleagues and organised into teams.'

'Before that, could everyone who has taken a seat, please get up and walk to the back of the church.'

There is a delay as the people in the pews get to their feet and shuffle their way towards me.

Philip waits till they are all gathered there and then, pauses further for dramatic effect. He is clearly enjoying his role.

'When the door opens could you all quickly leave. You have not been selected. Goodbye.'

There is a collective gasp from the room, which subsides into low groan from those at the back of the room. The chosen ones are silent but wide-eyed with relief.

Sammie catches my eye. I nod to the intense young man who walked past me earlier and is still at the fringes of the group, standing next to a camera furthest from the pulpit.

I rise and walk over to him. I smile, as he belatedly catches my eye. He offers me his hand as I move close. I slowly shake my head, the thin smile never leaving my face and say:

'I'm sorry Ben but you're out too.'

32: BANALITY SHOW

The next person to be ejected causes more of a scene. Her name is Diana. I remember her name and face from her picture. She is an attractive middle-aged woman, who dressed in her picture as today, perhaps just a little too young for her age. But even so she carries herself well and has a certain poise and presence.

She is clearly used to carrying her own way in the face of opposition and is the only one of the candidates to argue when Philip tells them that we will not be answering any questions about the nature of The Group or the selection day.

Her voice is strident and precise and conveys supreme self-confidence. 'Don't be so ridiculous. How can we possibly demonstrate that we are best suited to whatever it is you have in mind, if you don't tell us what it is you are looking for?'

When Philip moves away from the pulpit to see who has spoken, he immediately seems short and flustered. The mystique of control begins to slip. He manages to say: 'We know what we are looking for,' but his voice sounds weak and ineffectual in comparison to hers.

'You may well do, but remember we might not think that it is quite so important as you do. Some of us have better things to do than waste time on silly little games.'

She is impressive. I am immediately drawn and attracted to her. The natural authority in her voice makes the rest suddenly aware of their own passivity. I can almost see them thinking 'Why should we put up with this artificial situation? Who is this silly little man?'

Philip is angered and intimidated by her and in danger of losing it entirely.

I speak up from the back of the church before things can go any further.

'Diana, all you need to know is that if you don't want to be here you can leave,' I say to her, and then to the rest of the Group: 'I don't want to waste anyone's time, so anyone who wants to waste ours with questions that will not be answered, leave now – so who is going to join Diana on the way out?'

There is a small pause before it becomes clear that no one is going to step out of line to join her. Left isolated by The Group, Diana still manages to maintain her poise.

'Well if you're looking for sheep, it looks like you've found them.'

She turns and walks for the door with a measured sway to her hips, her heels beating out time on the hard stone floor. I watch as people hang their heads and look away.

There are thirty-four people left, all eager to comply. Some of them expect to be rejected, some have blind faith, the rest simply give it their best.

We organise them into four roughly equal teams. The mix is still pretty good, but there is a definite skew towards youth and vitality. The older members begin to fade into the background, beaten by time.

We lead them into the church hall, where PMC rehearse their teen bands. We have them carry the video cameras into the large brightly lit room that is lined with mirrors. The overall impression is that they will all be watched, exposed and examined.

Some wilt under the scrutiny, others rise to the challenge. As tasks are organised and filmed, leaders soon emerge, personalities become apparent.

I have them perform routines, compete physically with their opposing teams, make impassioned pleas to camera to see who is most willing to go where we tell them and do as we say.

I then have them nominate one member from their group as leader and another for expulsion. A tired and familiar routine, but embraced ruthlessly by those willing to fight hardest, even when ignorant of the prize.

By mid afternoon we have fifteen people and then ten and by the end of the long, exhausting day, our final five. And I can watch no more.

The five that stand before us at the end are jubilant, screaming with naked joy and mock disbelief. They hug each other with fake togetherness, jumping up and down in genuine victory.

There are three girls and two boys. All young and flawless. And later when I review the tapes, I cannot tell them apart because their faces are so hard.

33: SAMMIE

I have abdicated almost all daily responsibility to the inner circle of helpers. Asako and Jun are now fully committed, Philip gives the impression of having taken charge, but I sense that Sammie is the quiet power behind the throne.

How remarkable. Sammie a man, little more than a

boy, ten weeks ago, timid, passive, invisible. A slight figure, with a forgettable boyish face, pale china skin and grey eyes. Nothing, nobody. And now this. How can he have come so far?

I rely upon him for everything now. He is the lynchpin that runs my team at Silverback by day and The Group by night.

At work he has made startling progress with the mish-mash team he now leads. They are now more than a forgotten add-on, and instead are hitting their stride, expanding their business model, aiming at interesting and important work.

I'm not entirely sure how this has all happened. If I'm honest, I have to admit I'm a little bit perturbed by the extent of their progress after I relinquished control.

To me they seemed like such a lost cause but Sammie seems to have turned them around without wasting any energy on unnecessary emotion. He's just shown a calm acceptance of his situation coupled with a still determination to get things done.

I wonder if I could have achieved similar had I tried.

He is the same in our other project. He has become a beacon within the The Group, where previously we had no centre. There are no sweeping plans, or agitated questions. There is none of the performance that can often be found when people work together. He simply takes each step as he finds it, and we all try to follow.

And despite all this, he still looks to me. I am his catalyst, which gives me an enormous degree of satisfaction, even pride.

I prefer not to think too much about it but feel that

when I started all this it was born out of a sense of desperation. A blind need to halt the slide in my life, and jolt myself out of cruise control.

I suppose that my willingness to act without precisely knowing what I was doing is no different from those in The Group. We all want something more, without really knowing what or why. A more positive person may even see my actions as my opting back into life, taking charge and being enthusiastic and all that other preppy prozac stuff.

But I don't know if I can truly believe that to be so. The truth is probably more like I was terminally bored and needed do something. Anything. And rushing headlong into it with people beside me following my lead has been a blinding rush.

Where this'll end up, I'm not sure. I am again feeling the pressure to come up with something big and amazing for the five to do. I need vision and genius, I need to be a leader of men. What a joke.

Whatever happens though, one good thing is clear, and that is the emergence of Sammie. As I see his achievements add up by the day, I know that however things turn out, I have shaped something real in him.

Something I can be proud of.

34: THE GROUP

The chosen five: Sarah, blonde, 19, perky, fresh, wholesome, clean.

Nikki, 22, blonde, peroxide, black roots, harder-edged, spiky pouty, slutty, meant to look dirty, small, petite but somehow manages to look much bigger on screen.

Sharonne, 23, kinky chocolate hair, mixed-race, urban, hip, with a touch of the nu-soul, rootsy, funk mother.

Charlie, 17, posh, plummy, ruddy, unfeasibly tall, spiky hair, clumsy, awkward, good bloke, very, very earnest.

Jonas, 25, boot-polish black-dyed hair, androgynous, retro, tight jeans, not afraid of leather or make-up. Camp, skinny, pale, pale skin, slightly sickly, junkie rock-star look, but well within the bounds of acceptability.

All very different, all extremely compliant.

We call them in for a conference in Philip's office. I can see that they are confused and disoriented by their surroundings but there are no questions. Their sense of discomfort is heightened by the video cameras that are again trained on them.

They have been told nothing about what they have been chosen for but this doesn't deter them. We tell them they have a week to back out of The Group, but once they are in, they are in. They must abide by the rules and we retain copyright, in the UK and worldwide in perpetuity.

They have already been told not speak to anyone about their selection. We now tell them that if anything breaks in the press, all five will be immediately rejected, regardless of whether the leak can be traced back to them or not.

We tell them not to tell boyfriends, girlfriends, best friends or family. We tell them that ninety percent of celebrity stories are leaked to the tabloids by people the celebrities thought they could trust.

The message is stay smart, keep your mouths shut and don't blow your chance.

The five are wide-eyed but thrilled to hear that they

are now the subjects of potential press attention.

They each dream their secret dreams that I can only think are depressingly uniform. Flash-bulbs popping, interviews, autographs, groupies, endorsements, red carpets, premieres, parties and of course, the acceptance of other celebs. A cotton-candy world, soft, fluffy and sickly sweet.

And then, while they are all glassy-eyed and deep in their individual narcotic fantasies, Philip hits them with the kicker.

'The next time we see you, you will have given up your current lives. Jobs, education, girlfriends, boyfriends, fiancés, husbands, wives, friends, flatmates, where you live, where you go out, your musical tastes, your dress sense, your opinions, all gone.'

'If you want to back out you have a week to decide. But if you're in we own you for the next year. We'll have documents ready for you to sign.'

The five are silent. Staring at their shoes. Licking dry lips. Glancing up at us and each other. I expect some protest. From Jonas, from Sharonne, from Charlie, from any one of them.

Nothing. No contest. They are ours to do with as we want.

35: PUNCHLINES

There are times when even I know that a joke has been taken too far.

I hear from Sammie that Gemma has been sacked. And humiliated.

She's been having an affair with a client. A married

client. An older man with a digital camera.

A series of grainy anatomical snapshots and tired clichéd emails has been sent to all. And then sent on. And on. And on.

The details are sketchy but both Gemma (kinky b*tch) and (the now ex-) client (naughty boy) initially turned on each other when the indiscreet emails first turned up in a hundred eager inboxes.

But it soon became clear that neither of them had mistakenly sent the email.

A virus is the new prime suspect. Web security experts have been called in. New email policy announced. And Gemma has gone. No one knows where. No one really cares.

A virus? I'm not so sure. More likely a disgruntled employee.

Seven days.

I can feel the others waiting.

For me to come up with something.

For The Group.

So many useless ideas. So few original thoughts.

I am alone with my madness.

I feel the pressure.

Desperate. Anxious.

Exposed.

And the only thing I can think is: sometimes you really can take a joke too far.

36: I BET YOU THINK THIS SONG IS ABOUT YOU

Torrid is bankrolling The Group, and Philip wants to know what his money is buying.

He wants to know what I have in mind.

He calls every day.

Impatient. As always.

Scheming. I think.

I can't stall forever. Or I'll lose control. The cards will collapse and fall all around me.

And I'll lose my place.

I psyche myself up.

I have nothing ready. But I call them altogether.

Forcing myself on.

We meet back at the church hall. It feels strangely quiet.

The others are there before me. Waiting.

I try to make myself think: 'It's ok. These are your friends. Things will fall into place.'

But it does nothing to quash the feeling that it's actually me versus them. The dread I'm feeling is making my chest tingle. I feel paralysed.

But I'll have to say something now that I'm here.

'Errm. Hello everyone. Glad you're all here. Good to see you all. How have you all been?' I ask rather lamely.

Jun and Asako seem to have sensed the strange tension in the room and smile nervously, bobbing their heads up and down at speed in attentive Japanese style.

Sammie is still.

Typically, Philip goes at it like a bull in a china shop.

'Yeah, yeah we're all fine. So what's happening? We've got the kids. They look good. I think we've done well. But now it's all gone quiet. We need to move. So what's it to be? Made your mind up yet? Ready to share the masterplan?'

'Philip, I can understand your impatience but there is really no need to rush. Things are falling into place. Taking shape. We have to let it develop and allow it to become what it is.'

Philip looks at me, and then at Sammie. He looks at the floor, takes a deep breath and then looks at Asako, who gives him the slightest of nods.

I'm sure of it now, they are sleeping together and poor old Jun knows nothing about it. I feel a twinge of anger and then shame. I know that I am no better than Philip myself, and certainly no better than Asako with her brightly polished ambition.

'Khaled, I hear what you are saying. I'm not questioning your judgement, but we need to know more. What are we trying to achieve here?' asks Philip.

'Nothing at all, Philip, nothing at all. Not in the way you mean. I just want to show you what people will do in the name of a common cause. How they perform and exceed all expectations when they feel part of something.'

'But what does that mean exactly? What does that prove? I understand the way we've been able to manipulate people into doing things that they would normally not do, and I understand that that can feel powerful, but what's the point unless you have something else in mind. You've got to get them to do something worthwhile, for it to be really meaningful.'

Asako is nodding away. I look directly at her as I speak. 'I'm not really sure you do understand Philip. But you must know how easy it is to tap into the unsavoury part of someone's character. You understand how little it takes to get someone to lie, cheat, betray if they think there's something in it for them at the end. Even when they have no idea what the prize is, they'll still do things they'd rather not talk about, won't they?'

Asako is flushed and biting her lip, but Philip has no idea what I'm talking about. He interrupts me:

'Khaled, that's the point, no one does know what the prize is. Wouldn't it be clearer if we made some decisions now? If you're just trying to show us how you can lead people on, then you've already done that. I mean how far do you want to take it? If these kids show up again, they've agreed to give up their entire lives without any idea of what they getting involved in – doesn't that prove your point?'

I say nothing and wait for him to reveal his hand. When he speaks again it is in a far more conciliatory tone.

'Look Khaled, I can see that you're onto something, I just want to find some way to harness it, find some kind of application. You've brought us this far, which is amazing really but maybe it's time to put our heads together. Otherwise what are we going to do with these kids? Play games with them?'

'Ok Philip, what do you have in mind, let's hear it?'

'Well, you know, actually, I have had a few ideas. The five we have are the perfect template for a pop group. I know the industry, I know people who can polish them in to a perfect little package, we can sign them to PMC, or one of the other majors and Torrid can take care of the marketing push. We could really make something of these guys, change their lives and you know, we could change our lives at the same time, make some money, the whole thing. Now what's wrong with that?'

I stay silent. It's no real surprise that this is the grand scheme that Philip and Asako have mapped out.

'The other thing is, you'd be suited to it, Khaled. You'll enjoy it. I mean at least half of promoting a pop group is hype, convincing people to go along with the idea that the group is something really special, when 99% of the time, it's really not. But people still fall for it, time after time. Isn't that part of what you are trying to do?'

As he speaks, my tension and uncertainty fade. I begin to realise something. There is a calm clarity to my thinking. Everything has suddenly snapped together, and I can see the whole and can articulate it. Now that Philip has said the unthinkable, I really don't know why I got cold feet or became so hesitant. His is the kind of thinking that got me here in the first place

I know what it is that I'm here to do. And when I speak, it is with total belief.

'No Philip, that's got nothing at all to do with what I'm trying to do. You're talking about some glossy scam to make money out of infatuated little girls. I'm trying to show the world what we have become. I'm trying to show people that we are being processed, packaged and fed into a machine. And the sad thing is we do it willingly. We are not people, or a society, we're components. If you manipulate conditions in a certain way, you get a certain response. We're all victims of the same thing, even you

Philip, even you the master manipulator. And me. There's always something else we are looking for, because what we have is so deeply unsatisfying. And you know what? It doesn't have to be that way. Each one of us has the potential to be productive, satisfied, happy, content but we're not. None of us. Very few of us release our potential, because all our energy goes into maintaining the machine. Belonging to the group. Conforming. Accepting. Fitting in. Belonging. All that potential subverted, perverted, warped and channelled into narrow little tracks that we call career or lifestyle. We're being controlled by our own desires, and those desires have been hacked into. We don't even know what we want anymore, we are force-fed contrived needs and cancerous insecurities that only serve us to make us scared, malleable and oh so docile. And you know what? I don't want that, I want nothing to do with it.'

I pause and look at Philip with compassion in my face and I know him as my brother. Asako is my sister. They both hear what I'm saying and see what I see.

'All I want to do now is show people how it works and then it's their choice. And you know what? I can't say if what I'm trying to show them is right or not. I don't know if it is less painful to belong to the group, to stomach all the daily indignities in exchange for the warmth of acceptance or take the lonely path, where we each try to find out what we really are. I can see now that, the greatest trick of all, is that every one of us already thinks we are free. As if we have earned that right. We each believe that our lives belong to us and that we are all special, all worthy of barren praise and a sickly attention that feeds itself and has become an end in its own right. And the ultimate result of this sweet deception is that we conform. Our behaviour can be predicted, measured and fed back into the machine. A machine that sustains us like a father and a mother. I don't know, I really don't know. It's almost impossible to put into words. But it is there. A creeping feeling that's all too real. And I know there are many, many people out there who feel the same way, as if they are being expertly hustled out of something every single day. They have the same nagging doubts that I do. And all I want to do is speak to them and show them they may be right to listen to those doubts. And that's enough, that's all I want to do. And this thing, this thing of ours, if we really want to do something significant or important, or meaningful, it's just one way of showing them. That's enough, it really is, The rest is up to them.'

I stop talking. There is silence. There are tears in my eyes. I look from face to face, Asako gentle and beautiful, Jun my friend, thoughtful, kind. Philip, calm and focused, blessed with great energy.

And then I turn to Sammie, the unsung and uncomplicated ally who I have come to depend on. I smile as the tears find my face.

He looks at me evenly. His unblinking eyes are more eloquent than what he says:

'Actually I agree with Philip. The pop group; that's what we're going to do.'

37: THE OPPOSITE OF KNOWING

When I was a child, from about the age of nine to twelve, I remember the women who filled my house with gossip, morality and cautionary tales. My mother, her two aunts, one deaf and nimble who lived two doors away, the other, her sister, who had a kindly face, but one marked by the loss of her unruly hard-drinking husband, who lived two hundred yards away to the other side of our house, and their eldest sister, my grandmother, fat and laughing, who slept me upon her belly, and fed me with sweets and carefully burnt aloo parotha, thickly buttered or white bread egg sandwiches (the yolk always broken and mixed up specially for me) and gold top milk, when left in her care on frosty early weekend mornings when my parents went off to work.

They would gather at my mother's house, drinking sweetly spiced milky tea and make me dizzy with all the odd sounding names of their people and places. Subidarni, from the village of Khala Singia, who married Bhuta Sau, and had three children, the eldest of whom, Bubbli, lived in Derby and had had six children herself, but none of them boys.

The difference between a Chacha and a Mama, a Sass and a Nau. Something to with which side of the family they come from: your uncle on your mother's side or your father's sister, never really explained, but something you were expected to know. I just liked the sound of the words, and made precocious jokes, mocking the tales of high operatic melodrama that filled our front room before the men came home to be fed and obeyed.

So when the women told the tale of Bibi Tanti whose joon or life had been ruined by her no good children, I would pipe up and say that these women were ruining my joon and my July.

And when my grandmother would curse in her coarse, colourful, unread way, saying he is as worthless as the ash from seven outdoor ovens, or that he is as crooked as dog's tail, which you can keep held straight in a pipe for twelve years, but will still come out bent, I would shriek with delight and plead for more coarse phrases from the soil of the old country.

I remember how they would sit, three sisters who often had rivalries of their own and my mother. How they would judge. Such and such is no good, she doesn't keep her house clean, she's lazy, she doesn't know how to make tea even, and the poor husband is such a good boy, he works late for the family and when he returns home, there is no food on the table and his own children spit in his face.

And I would believe every vivid word, knowing that there is good and bad in the world and no in between. An easy equation that would comfort and soothe.

And I remember one story they told more often than most. The tragic story of a mother's sacrifice, a woman of their own generation, who came to this country in the same wave as them. A saintly lady, simple in her ways, uncomplicated, uneducated, but respectable and true.

How she worked. Keeping her home together. Then after the death of her husband, taking on other people's cleaning. The shame, the silent dignity, the suffering. Keeping her son in school. One of the first of their generation to see her son go on to university.

The son became what my bibi, my grandmother, described as an officer, meaning a man of status, when he finally graduated as a doctor. And he continued to progress in the gora's world, despite all the hostility and the obstacles, to become one of the first hospital consultants from our people.

But he committed the ultimate betrayal, he forgot his roots. Disregarded our traditions. Thought he was better than us, better than his poor long suffering mother. He married a white woman. He had mixed race children. Left his mother with the taste of ash and shame in her mouth.

And again the old woman showed courage and dignity. She disowned her son, refused to acknowledge his wife, and even her own grandchildren, knowing in her heart that the women, the ones like my mother, my grandmother, my aunts, their friends, and all the others like herself, would talk and talk about her scornful son.

The inevitable happened: the evil sorceress divorced the wayward son. His children spat in shame at this brown-skinned man, knowing nothing of his ways. And he was left with nothing, no ties to his roots, no family of his own, the ultimate punishment, but fitting for a man who showed such folly.

That's the way the women told it. The break-up gave the story legs; it ran for years and years. The saintly old woman, and her educated son who thought he knew too much. The women took great solace and glee from that story, and it was heady stuff for a boy of nine, who knew nothing but the ways of his house and his family and the rules by which we lived our lives, and defined ourselves as different.

But as you grow, you see things that make you

uncomfortable. Good, obedient Indian boys, many of them in their thirties or forties, with families of their own, who do not act in the way the women say. But they are not scorned in the way of the wayward son.

And you see that the great idea of our people, family and extended family, the Indian virtue, is not so great or strong after all. Brothers falling out with brothers when money and business become an issue. But still they are blameless in the eyes of the women, it is always the work of new wives or outsiders who plot and scheme.

And you realise that, as you grow older still, that the old ways may not be right for you. You feel the pressure of the new world opening up and old duties pulling you back. You don't want to be like the wayward son. You don't want to betray your people, who gave everything for you, but you start to see how he might have felt, when you realise nothing you do will ever make up for the fact that you are not the same as them.

You sense their fear and uncertainty in the new place. A place they have lived in for thirty, forty, fifty years. A place where they will die, but never call home. A place that infects them and marks them as different when they go back to the mother that they do still call home. The mother that scorns them and their children. Disowning them forever.

And you know then, that there never were any old ways. Just the fear of not knowing how things really work.

A gift that I still carry with me.

38: BREAKING IT DOWN

I wonder if this what a nervous breakdown feels like. I'm only getting a couple of hours fitful sleep at night. The rest of the night my mind is racing one anxious thought after another. One minute I'm incredibly relieved to have this nightmare taken away and so I'll be consumed by a panicky laughter that leaves me breathless, empty and more than a little scared.

And then there is anger and arrogance. 'Who the fuck is Sammie? I made that bitch.'

Winding myself up into a teeth-grinding fury and frustration, self-consciously pulling my wall punches just enough so as not to truly hurt my hand.

But mostly there's guilt and self-pity, which I can't turn into a pantomime. I just want to turn off the lights, pull a duvet over my head and disappear. Forever.

The phone has been ringing. And my mobile's out of juice. But I don't care. I've seen Jun at the flat. He's tried knocking on my door a few times, but he seems embarrassed to be around me and I'm aggressive-defensive, not needing anyone's help. Not able to face anyone like this.

Days pass, nights crawl by. I haven't washed. Or changed my clothes. The fridge is empty, but I'm still not ready to leave the house. I've run out of cigarettes but I'm chain-smoking the butts I fish out of the ash-tray, breaking them open and re-rolling the charred tobacco with grubby fingers.

I want to hit bottom. I need to feel punished. For my folly. For my inadequacy. I just want to feel something. For real. I want to know what to do next. But all I feel is tired and hungry and if there are any answers to be found they aren't in this flat.

There are so many things that eat away at me. They need to be resolved. But that'll mean having to face them one more time. I'll have to do it soon or skulk away.

Philip isn't returning my calls. Jun has disappeared away. He must be with Asako, I haven't seen either of them at the flat for a couple of days.

Which leaves Sammie. I call him at the office, and put the phone down when he picks up. He's still going in. I have this sense that he knows it was me calling. I can't shake the idea that he can see through me at all times and now that I've let him know I'm coming, he'll be ready.

I don't think there is much I can do now, but I have to try to end this.

39: KRS-ONE

I need to get ready. My vacation's over. I'll wash. Shave away the beard. Have my haircut. Have my suit dry-cleaned and shirt washed and ironed. Polish my shoes. Dig out my cuff-links. Assemble the uniform. But first I need to eat.

I feel nervous and on display. Like a trespasser. I haven't been to the office for so long, I'm sure people will want some kind of explanation, show surprise to see me or want know where I've been, and I don't know what to say for myself.

I keep expecting someone to stop me on the way in. Or pull me to one side as I use my security card to open the door to the office. I'm waiting for someone to grab me as I float past desks and glass-enclosed offices. It's strange and surreal like a dream where I can be seen but not noticed.

So I reach my desk without incident. Only Stefan is there. At least he looks surprised to see me.

I still can't think of anything to say, so I just ask the obvious.

'Hey Stefan, what's up? Where is everyone?'

'Errrm, they're out. I mean they're all in meetings.'

Silence.

'Uhm so err, how are you? I mean, are you back?'

'I'm fine Stefan. And yes I'm back. For now. So how have things been?'

'Really busy. Mad really. We've been winning loads of new work. Martin and Joe are at a pitch right now actually.'

'So things are going well?'

'Yeah really well. We're having to take on new staff. Sammie's been interviewing people. And there's a new girl who started this week, as his assistant.'

'Oh yeah? What's she like?'

'Her English isn't perfect, but she seems really good.'

'Is that right? Where's she from?

'I'm not sure but she looks Japanese.'

'Ok I see,' I say, thinking Asako certainly gets around.

'So where are they now?'

'They're with Philip and his pop band.'

'Are they at Torrid or at the church?'

'What?'

'Are they at Torrid's offices or at PMC's rehearsal space at the church?'

'Errm I'm not sure, but I don't think they'll be at PMC though. We're not really flavour of the month at PMC at the moment'.

'Why what's happened?'

'Someone from Silverback sent a release out, which was supposed to be from Torrid, which basically quoted someone from PMC saying that they don't waste time listening to the records they sell and that the Torrid system is so clever it can be used to minimise the random talent factor when it comes to selling an act. He said that he could see a day when PMC would be able to drop the pretence that a band actually has anything to do with music. He said all he needs is five tone-deaf, photogenic puppets to mime and dance around, a recycled hit and Torrid and he could guarantee a number 1.'

'Fucking hell, who wrote that?' I ask, genuinely taken aback.

'Well no one knows. Someone just sent it out, no one knows anything about it and the person at PMC is just a made up name. They hit the roof. So did Torrid, but Sammie reckons Philip is probably secretly loving it.'

'So what happened?' I ask, thinking Philip probably would relish every minute.

'Well PMC are threatening to sue and Torrid have dropped Quentin's team and they're refusing to pay him.

If it wasn't for Sammie, they'd have dropped Silverback altogether, so that's won our team some points.'

'What happened with the story?' I ask.

'It went out to about fifty journalists but luckily no one picked up on it, otherwise we'd have been in deep shit.'

'A story like that? And no one picked it up? Fucking hell,' I say, thinking I really don't know anything at all.

'Yeah lucky or what?'

'Yeah. Lucky. And no one knows who sent it out?'

'It definitely went out from Silverback, on the right headed paper and all that, with all the right contacts, but it wasn't approved by anyone. It's sabotage basically. No one knows who did it.'

A thought enters my mind. 'What was the name of the person quoted at PMC?'

'I can't remember, but it sounded like a made up name. Funny sounding.'

'Can you look it up somewhere?'

'Well we're not supposed to have seen the release, but it was sent round the office, I think I've still got it in my inbox.'

I wait for him to find it and I already know what I'm going to hear.

'Here it is,' he says. 'Hold on let me find his name. Yeah, here we go. Arturo Blisset. Got to be made up. No one's heard of him here, Torrid or PMC.'

'I've heard of him,' I say, as I walk away with a small smile, thinking maybe I do know just a little bit.

Just nothing worth knowing.

40: FRIENDS AND FAMILY

From the outside of the church hall, looking in through the windows I can see Asako. She is standing with her back to me, facing the brightly coloured members of the group I chose.

They are sitting on stools in a semicircle around her, listening intently, nodding their heads, mouths shut, seldom speaking. They already look so different from the last time I saw them. Their clothes and hair much stagier and more styled. Their individual characteristics have been heightened, so that each represents an artist's impression of a demographic type, but strangely they manage somehow to look more alike then they ever did before. Neither male or female, or black or white, just somewhere in between.

But I have to remember, somewhere underneath the air-brushed layers of their new look, they are still the same five kids I lied to, who deserve to be told the truth.

As I walk round to the door. I see Philip walk into the hall, with Sammie and someone else I can't make out. The sight of them hits hard: a pick and mix of emotions. Fear. Anger. Panic. But mainly sadness. I'm not part of their unit anymore and I miss the excitement.

Sammie casually turns away from the other two, lifting his head so his gaze rests directly upon me. There is no surprise in his eyes, he just nods his head once, and then turns back to face Philip and the other man.

Philip is first to react when I open the door to the church hall. He turns towards me open mouthed, takes a couple of steps forwards and then rather predictably starts screaming: 'What fuck are you doing here? Get the fuck out. There's nothing for you here. Fuck off.'

I'm still framed in the doorway, yet to enter the room, but Philip is furious. His face and eyes are red and bright and his thick little neck is bulging as he strains his vocal cords. He's spitting saliva, the veins on his temple glow almost green with frustration because his words are soon choked off and strangled, as he's no longer capable of forming sentences. He appears to be having a seizure.

I miss him so much.

The kids are wide-eyed and open-mouthed at Philip's outburst. For some reason Rhys is here; he's the third man that I couldn't quite place through the window. Seeing him here is so unexpected, it almost causes me to giggle out loud through nerves and tension. He cowers back as Philip works himself up to a crescendo.

But despite his fury and aggression, I can see that Philip is rattled by my presence. He looks from me to Sammie and then back at me with wild uncertain eyes. Sammie's definitely the man in charge now. As if there was ever any doubt.

'Hello Khaled,' he says. 'Don't mind Phil. He's just excited to see you.'

I am the outsider again. Asako and the five members of The Group have managed to edge away to the furthest corner of the room, away from the commotion. Rhys is left by himself, awkwardly staring at his shoes and I'm left facing Sammie, who is flanked by Philip, still clearly agitated, eyes rolling, tongue flicking out over his thick lips, hands flexing open and shut. It seems that only Sammie can look at me.

I'm losing my nerve with every passing second. The moment is frozen between Sammie and me. He has a small satisfied smile that I have never seen before. I have to speak before he paralyses me.

'Can we go for a walk?' I ask.

'Sure, let's go.'

Philip steps towards me, but Sammie motions him to stay, with the smallest shake of his head. He gives the impression of someone who wears his power well. I can only admire him.

We walk in silence from the church hall to the church itself. The sky is bluish grey and there is a cold moisture in the air. A mulchy carpet of leaves; some red, some yellow, some brown, litter the path we walk upon, sticking to our shoes and muffling the sound of our passing.

I can see squirrels dashing between the trees. I can see black ravens hopping on the lawn. And in the cloudless sky, the silhouette of a great plane draws an effortless line against the dark grey of distant tower blocks.

My ears are cold and my lips are cracked. But I'm alive. And I have nothing to fear.

Without any sunlight to illuminate the windows, the church is a lifeless, empty shell. Grey and gloomy, with none of the spark and crackle of the first time I was here.

Sammie stamps his feet and walks along the aisle to the front of the church, to stand below the great carved figure of Christ, which is now indistinct and lifeless in the shadows.

He turns and leans against the pulpit. From the back of the church, he seems so small. The thought of attacking him flashes briefly through my mind. But only very briefly. I've seen him in action, and I know I have no experience of violence. The last thing I need is further confirmation of the pecking order.

'So Khaled, what do you want?'

'You know, Sammie, I've never been able to answer that. I'm always ready to spout my useless opinions and advice for other people, but completely unprepared when it comes to deciding anything for myself. But you know what? I think it's about time I made up my mind.'

'That's very interesting Khaled. But let's stick to the point shall we? Why are you here now? What specifically do you want?'

'I want you to stop. With The Group. At least, I want you to stop with what you're doing. Maybe there is something else we can do with them, something more in line with what I originally thought.'

'No. That's not going to happen. And there isn't any 'we' or 'us'. You're not part of this anymore.'

'But I started it Sammie. It was all me. Without me there wouldn't be anything at all. You know that. Of all people you should know that.'

'You started something Khaled, I'll give you that. But that doesn't make it yours to do with as you want. This is bigger than you now. It's gone far beyond you. And like you're always so fond of saying, I don't think you ever had a clear idea of what you wanted anyway. I do and that's what's going to happen.'

'Ok Sammie, so you know what you want. But I showed you how to get it. I mean look at you now. You're magnificent. I just want you to remember where you were six months ago'.

'No Khaled, I don't want to remember that at all. And looking at you does remind me.'

'So you don't feel you owe me anything at all? Really? You don't remember how I trusted you? How I gave you the room to become what you are now. You don't want to remember any of that?'

Sammie's voice finally shows emotion, but all I can hear is anger: 'You didn't make me, you needed me. You relied upon me to get things done,' he shouts. 'You were lucky you had me, and the rest of us. We made this, while you were wanking off, trying to discover yourself. Yeah, you needed us, but we didn't need you. I don't need you.'

'You're right. You don't need me. You've got it all worked out I'm sure. You and Philip. And those kids. I guess I'm just an embarrassing reminder of something a little less slick and well worked out. But we all get taken in a little bit don't we? Even you. And you know what? I did trust you. And maybe this is patronising, but I was also very proud of you. I still am. And I thought you were my friend.'

Sammie turns away from me, stiff-backed, silent.

'Sammie?'

'Look,' he says in a quiet voice once again, 'I'll admit that you helped me, but we were never friends. I was like your prize poodle, performing loyal little tricks at your command. And there's no way I'm going back to that. Ok?'

I stay quiet. Not wanting to give him an easy way out.

'And I'm not giving up The Group. You might've started it, but it's mine now. Alright?'

I say nothing at all, waiting to see what he'll offer.

'I built The Group. I worked at it. I made it all happen. It's more mine than it ever was yours. And I took it away from you. And there's no way you're getting it back, to throw it all away.'

I continue to wait patiently for him to gather his thoughts.

'Listen, you didn't know what you wanted to do with The Group anyway. It was all a big joke to you. So you haven't lost anything. I'm going to be leaving Silverback, I'll make sure you can walk back into your old job. The team's doing a lot better now than it used to, and that's all my work. You take that, and I'll take the thing you started. That's fair. An exchange so you won't lose anything. Chalk it up to experience, Khaled. And if you have any other projects that are bit more thought out and a bit better commercially realised, you can always talk to me. How does that sound?'

The longer I stay quiet, the more he has to think about things and the more uncomfortable he seems,

'Listen you fucker. Don't try that silent treatment on me. You're not getting anything else out of me. This is your only chance. You better fucking say something or you can disappear.'

'Ok Sammie, I'll speak. Like I said before, it's time to

make up my mind. Do I want to go back to Silverback? Not really. Do I want to bring you some other project? I don't think so. Why am I here? Well a bit of me feels angry at you. And disappointed. I think what you're doing now is bullshit. You may not like it, but I saw something in you, and I think you're making a mistake. You could do something so much better. But, that's up to you. I have to realise what people like you want to do with their lives is nothing to do with me. Do I want anything to do with The Group? You're right, you put more into it than me, and you have some sort of clear idea of what you want to do with it, even though I don't agree with it. So if I'm really honest, I don't want that either. Which leaves me with your last choice. I could disappear. That sounds pretty good to me right now.'

Sammie turns back to face me.

'Ok so go,' he says. 'I'll make sure you can take away some money from Silverback, and from Torrid. Don't say no. You'll need it.'

'Ok. But I want to go with a clear conscience. I need to tell those kids the truth. Then I'm gone, forever.'

'Ok. You can tell them whatever you want. They belong to me now'.

41: THANKS - BUT NO THANKS

There are many types of hero. There are the talented and the beautiful. The determined and the brave. We admire them, but mostly we celebrate what they stand for: Success.

But then there are also the tragic heroes. The ones that do what they have to do without any hope of triumph or victory. They were always the ones that fascinated and moved the innocent child I once was.

I would waste many naïve hours by myself as a gangly, too tall, pre-teen kid, working out various elaborate fantasies that would always revolve round my romantic sacrifice in the face of insurmountable odds. I loved the idea of making a futile gesture.

And as important as the idea of living life with a set of unshakeable convictions was, there was no denying the cloying notion that my pure actions would somehow shame my unworthy peers. In my mind they'd barely be able to look at my battered, bloody and cheerfully dying body but they'd be forced to acknowledge the unbroken nature of my spirit to the very end.

Of course life's not like that, and there's nothing worse than the romantic who turns cynic, but how else are we to mark ourselves out as different from the crowd, when we realise we don't have the guts to be idealists?

Then there'd be other fantasies, horribly common it turns out, that I was someone extremely special. Unique in fact, and that this stage, all that appears to be real, was constructed just for me. And I'd be a prince or an alien of kind. An experiment gone wrong. Forced into hiding for my own safety. Or constantly tested and surveilled, without my knowledge. Everything around me unreal, a set and all the people actors.

But you know, I could always tell something wasn't right. The first feelings that somehow that this couldn't be it or that I didn't quite fit in. Feelings that I was destined for other things, but again not without a noble struggle that would see my true nature transcend my surroundings.

Embarrassing in a way to look back upon, but also painful to think about what I've lost. Or what I might have been.

There will never be a better moment than when I walked back through the doors of the church hall ahead of Sammie to face the people that my actions have brought together and united.

I look into all their faces. They are uncertain and confused. As if not sure what has happened between me and Sammie. Fearing the worst. More shouting. Violence. Fearing, perhaps, an accommodation that will see my return to lead them where none of them want to go.

Anxious expectancy in all their faces. In the flat shiny faces of The Group, who don't want to hear what I have to say, because it will jeopardise their fragile dreams. In the face of Asako who knows all that I know about her. In the face of Philip, who has openly scorned me, burning all his bridges, leaving him no politic manoeuvre by which he can remain with me and still save face. Even in the face of incongruous Rhys who has no idea who I am or what I have done.

Even Jun, who is the simplest, most honest person here, is looking back at me with trepidation and discomfort, which is the clearest sign that I am swimming against the tide. And that I am wrong. There is no reason to denigrate what they are doing; it just isn't for me.

'Hello everyone,' I say. 'It really is nice to see you again. I really shouldn't have left you in the way that I did.'

Silence. Nerves. A small trace of a smile on Jun's lips.

'I went away because I couldn't really cope with what was happening, but I'm back now. Back to myself anyway but I won't be sticking around. My heart's not really in it.'

There is visible relief on some faces. Jun looks away.

'I also owe you another more difficult apology. I manipulated and bullied you. And for no real reason other than to make myself feel good. I lost control of what I was doing very early and just got sucked into the whole idea of messing with people's lives. I don't know what to say really, it's difficult to admit, but my intentions were not pure or good or even very constructive. I need to make peace with that and find peace, so all I can say is I'm so very sorry.'

Jun looks extremely uncomfortable, he never was one for displays of emotion or self-flagellation. The rest just look bored. Philip even looks at his watch while I'm speaking. Never mind this isn't really for them. I'll cut to the chase.

'Ok, well that's more or less what I had to say. But before I go I just want to speak to you five,' I say, looking at The Group. 'I'm responsible for bringing you here and I helped pick you out and I just wanted to let you know what the real story is. Then you can decide for yourselves what you want to do.'

'Hold on, hold on,' says Philip, immediately sparking back to life. 'You've said your piece to us, but you've got nothing to say to them. Time to leave, Khaled.'

He's beginning to annoy me. I take a slow breath and try to stay Zen. I think personal sacrifice, nobility and insurmountable odds, but it's not easy.

Sammie steps out from behind me and speaks: 'It's ok Philip, this won't take long. Let him speak.'

'Thank you, Sammie,' I say. 'Do you think it might be possible to speak to them alone?'

Sammie lets out an exasperated sigh.

'Ok alright, we'll leave you alone. Five minutes, ok? We've got a lot to get on with,' he says. 'Ok, everyone out.'

'Thank you,' I say, smiling sweetly at Philip, who glares back at me as they all file past me to leave.

42: I TESTIFIED, MY MOMMA CRIED

So here it is finally. I'm face to face with the fruit of all my labours. They are a strange and unearthly crew. Five of them. A single unit.

So young. So beautiful. So rare and precious. To be gazed upon with awe and respect, beyond sexual attraction, like living artworks, perfectly displayed for one passing moment.

And yet so compromised. Willingly packaged to be pawed at and sold. Hungry. Visceral. Naked.

I stare at them and they stare at me. I know nothing about them. I assume everything I think I know. As does everyone they encounter.

I see attitude in Nikki. I see aggression in Jonas. I sense a vapid blankness in Charlie. I'm vaguely intimidated by the knowing look I see in Sharonne's face. And Sarah, or 'the other one' as she'll come to be known, simply fades into the background. But it is all just a reflex response. I have to tell myself that they are not what I see.

'You must be wondering what's going on. My name is Khaled and I started all of this.'

Once I've started, the minutes pass quickly and my confession is easy. I tell them I was bored, lost, unhappy, unfulfilled. I tell them how I would look at other people's lives with covetous eyes, and how I would lash out because I could never see a way of finding a life of my own. I tell them about the resentment that burnt so fiercely inside me. I tell them about the refuge I took venting my anger at others, without ever really knowing them. I tell them about the escape I found in lies. And the mania and the distraction I found in drawing people to me to manipulate them. I tell them that I never really knew what I was doing, but that it was hard to give up once I had started.

And then all too soon I have to tell them about the lie that brought them to this place and filled their heads with hope. I tell them that The Group was just a vicious joke. One designed to show how much people would endure for so very little. How it played on people's vanities and weaknesses. And how there never really was anything behind the ad that fooled so many people. That the whole thing was just a con, devised by me, so I could expose the cheap, venal nature of what we really are. Devised by me so that I too could feel special.

It's time to stop talking. I have very little left to say.

'I don't know what you've been told. By Sammie. Philip and the rest. But you ought to know the truth. That's why you're here. There is no pot of gold. They've got nothing to offer you. And we all lied to you from the very beginning. What you do now is up to you.'

I don't know what to expect really. Anger. Hostility. Tears. Shock. Laughter. Relief.

But there is nothing at all. I am invisible. Insignificant. They are staring right through me. Waiting to be switched on.

43: ARTURO

It turns out Sammie has already told them. One final joke, this time at my expense. Not so nice as it turns out.

He let them know there never was anything behind The Group. Just a prank. Hot air and chutzpah.

Sammie tells me this as he walks with me again, leading me away.

I ask him how they took it. I can't imagine it could have been easy.

'It wasn't difficult,' he says. ' At least not in the way you mean. The only difficult thing was convincing them I wasn't trying to trick them. Jonas seemed to think it was one more elimination test to catch them out. And the others seemed to believe him. They even started looking for hidden cameras. Even when they couldn't find one and they acknowledged what I was saying, they didn't really accept it. They seem to have developed a blind spot when it comes to facing up to things that they don't want to hear.'

'That's why we chose them I guess. Nothing's going to get in the way. Least of all the truth.'

'Maybe. Who knows? It was amazing listening to them though. Putting a positive spin on things. At first they were saying: "But you chose us. You must have seen something in us." And very soon they turned it around, convincing themselves that they had something special between them. Something self-sustaining. Saying things like "We've got a great energy in the group. A great look. Lots of talent. We can't waste this opportunity. Everyone who's made it has to get past hurdles in their career." And this was before I'd mentioned anything about a pop group or anything else for that matter. So you see Khaled. What you started, these kids, as you call them, are not so easy to control or manipulate. They're not so malleable as you think. They wouldn't have just blindly gone along with whatever you had in store for them. They want something for themselves. And they want it much more than you ever wanted anything yourself, and you can't argue with that. So believe me there's no way you would have got your way with them, they wouldn't have put up with any nonsense from you and if you'd tried that 'making a statement' line on them they'd have eaten you up for breakfast. At the end of the day you're not in their league Khaled.'

I'm slightly surprised to hear this from Sammie. But not shocked. I just can't engage with it enough. The oddest thing to me is actually how much he has said. The old Sammie I knew was solid and dependable, but extremely quiet and ever so hard to read, but now he seems to enjoy the sound of his own voice, and the wisdom of his own opinions. He's starting to sound like another self-important windbag I used to know, but I keep my thoughts to my self.

As I reach the gate that leads to the quiet tree lined road that will take me away from this place forever, I stop for a second and look at Sammie, offering him my hand.

He pauses for a second before taking it but then gives me the knuckle breaker.

'No hard feelings Khaled?' he asks.

'No. Not really. Good luck Sammie. I hope you get what you deserve.'

'No one gets what they deserve Khaled. They get what

they want hard enough to take. You should know that by now.'

I'm too tired to argue with him. He really is turning into a smug little monster. I'm glad I won't know him when he finally gets there.

Some movement catches my eye over his shoulder. It is Jun, Asako, and Philip skulking back to the church hall. And there, following them is the portly figure of Rhys. Incongruous. Out of place.

I can't help it, I have to ask before I go.

'What's Rhys doing here?'

'Rhys? You know he reminds me of you.'

'What?' I ask, genuinely surprised this time.

'Yes. I rescued him from Silverback. His talents weren't really appreciated in that place. It's a bit too literal and straight laced for someone like him.'

'You what? Are you sure? I worked with him. He's a total loser'.

'On the contrary, Khaled. He's very talented and imaginative. And there's one thing about him that I know you'll like: he doesn't follow the crowd, and he's certainly not scared to break a few rules.'

'Are we talking about Rhys here? The same Rhys that I used sit next to?'

'Yes Khaled,' says Sammie, 'I am talking about Rhys. But you might also know him as Arturo. That's what brought him to my attention.'

It's a savage punchline that leaves my head spinning. Who the hell knows anything I think. I start to laugh hysterically. Joyous. Shaking my head. Walking away.

44: FATHERS AND SONS

So things fall apart so easily and so quickly.

Jun is moving out. Asako only has a few months left on her student visa. They have decided to make a go of it, make the best of the time they have left together.

She moves fast and has already found a flat for them to move into. Jun has said that he is reluctant to leave me in the lurch, but I won't stand in his way. And his moving on will make it so much easier for me to leave.

The dark part of my soul tells me that she has always been prepared to take action to get what she wants. If I stayed, I wouldn't be surprised to see less and less of my old friend.

I also sense there may be marriage of convenience on the horizon. I'm not sure why, it's just a feeling. Maybe they'll try to track me down to send me an invitation, maybe they won't.

And after the requisite amount of time, she'll leave him either because she'll be safe from immigration or because she'll get tired of London.

Should I say something? Even if I knew what I was talking about, what would be the point really? And anyway I've got problems of my own.

Sammie has The Group (working title but one that seems to fit) on a school tour, keeping them busy, honing their skills, building that all-important pre-teen buzz for the band. They have no songs of their own yet but they are doing a kind of karaoke tour, covering recent hits.

I've heard from Jun that Philip is yet to decide between guitar-based teenie rock, or the safe banker of R'n'B urban-pop. We all know that look and image is crucial, but so is back-story, ready-made copy for all the press. So even without knowing what musical space they'll occupy, it is already clear who'll be the edgy one, who'll be the unofficial star of the band, who'll be touted as the real talent, and who'll be first to leave when sales are flagging and some last headlines are needed to drive the greatest hits collection.

Once all the details have been ironed out, the plan is to wheel out The Group in front of the all the big, the medium and then the small players in a series of industry showcases, but Jun thinks that PMC may have already locked down a deal.

Then it'll be Smash Hits, J17, daytime TV appearances, local radio, performances in shopping centres, touring way down the support bill, best newcomer award, a top-ten hit, cross branding, cross merchandising, electronic marketing, a number one, a slick tabloid-focused PR campaign, album sales, a tour of their own, glossier videos, talk of a more mature second album, talk of the band growing up, changing their image and the ride will go on for as long as it does before it all turns sour. And again things will all fall apart.

I guess I'll try to keep up with things from afar if I can but it'll have nothing to do with me anymore. Sammie has Philip, Philip has Asako, Asako has Jun, and I don't want any part of it.

So what's left?

I should feel jaded, cynical, twisted-up inside, bitter at my enemies, who were once my friends. But I don't.

I'm not interested in pop music, or clever marketing, or the intoxication of being associated with fame. And I don't wish to vent my spleen anymore at those people who are. That's just another distraction. And I don't need that.

They have their lives, I'll try to have mine.

I can see now that there was a point not so long ago where all I had inside me was a self-defeating ennui. Cold, intellectual, sneering with empty opinions and meaningless criticism of things and people I know nothing about, and have no right to judge.

How could this anaemic diet have sustained me for so long? But it couldn't keep me forever. Tipping point. I felt compelled to act. No procrastination, no thought, just action.

But without direction. Some vague notion about how people behave in groups, what they can be made to do, the idea of belief. Grandiose self-serving schemes about ego-art. Nothing crafted, simply media-savvy blag. Ultra-modern, uber-cool. Once again the copy writes itself.

God what on earth was I up to? But I'm left with some hope, because if I first thought without action, and then acted without thought, I eventually came to feel emotion, just at the point when it was all taken away from me.

So I have no job. But I cared nothing for what I did. I have no Group. But whichever way that went, I think it would have corrupted the person that I now hope to become. I have no friends, but the way I was going I would have pushed them away in some other way. So I've lost nothing. I've had a narrow escape and I have the journey ahead.

I put a call into my dad. To tell him my plans. I expect very little. But I can't just disappear.

'Dad.'

'Yes. Khaled? Is that you?'

'Yeah it's me. How are you Dad? How are things?'

'Alright. Everything is the same as it always is.How is your work?'

'Fine Dad, fine,' I say automatically without thinking. 'No Dad. I don't know why I said that. Work's not fine. It hasn't been for a long time. Listen Dad, don't say anything, but I've left.'

'What, you have left your job? What happened?'

'Nothing Dad. It's hard to explain. I just wasn't happy. I just needed to do something else.'

'So you just gave up your job? Because you weren't happy?'

'I didn't just give up the job, Dad, it's more complicated than that. I left for a while to do something else, and it didn't really work out, but it let me know that I can't go back to what I was doing before.'

'Ok you know best. So what are your plans now?'

'That's just it, Dad. I don't know what's best at all. I don't really have any solid plans.'

'Ok so take your time to decide.'

'Dad, there's one more thing. I'm leaving. I mean I'm leaving England. It's not a holiday. I'm leaving for good.'

I ready myself for the worst.

'Do you need money?'

'No Dad. I don't need any money. I'm not calling about money. Don't you want to know anything else? Like where I'm going or when?'

'You're not a child, Khaled. You're a grown man, I cannot question you. If you want to tell me you will.'

'Don't you care that I'm going? Don't you want to know what's happening with me?'

'Khaled. You are my son. But you need to stand on your own two feet. You've already said that you have no solid plans. You need to know what you want for yourself. And then you can tell me.'

'But don't you want to know where I'm going? Don't you want to stop me? Don't you want to say anything to me at all?'

'Khaled. You never give me a chance. Of course I want to know where you are going. And I want you to be safe and to tell me where you are and if you are coming back. But I don't want to stop you. You must do as you wish if you are to be happy. Do you want me to stop you?'

'No. It's not that. I just thought you wouldn't want me to go.'

'I don't want you to go Khaled. But if you must. You must. My father did not want me leave him. But it was necessary.'

'But you didn't have any choice. You had to leave.'

'Maybe it is the same for you. I don't know. Only you know that.'

'It's not the same. I don't have to go. I'm not doing it for my family. I'm deciding to go. It's my choice.'

'Khaled. I do not know what you want me to say to you. If you don't want to go, don't. Do you want me to forbid it? If I did would you listen? You are a man. You must decide for yourself. You are responsible for yourself. When I came to this country, it's true that I was able to help my family and my father, but he was not with me. I had to struggle for myself. And I was half your age Khaled. If you must do the same, I understand. I don't need you to do anything for me, so I have no say.'

'But I don't know what I'm going to do, Dad. I'm just going. I don't even know where.'

'You may have more choices that I had, but you must know that life is struggle Khaled. Life is struggle. If you don't struggle to succeed, everyday will be the same. I've had my struggle, those days are over for me, but what you choose is up to you. You can struggle to make something of yourself or you can just run away. That much is true wherever you are.'

'I think you might be right, Dad. Thank you. I'll let you know when I'm going and I'll keep in touch. I promise.'

'That is good. Khaled. I only wish the best for you my son. Goodbye.'

Someone must have called while I was speaking to my father. There is a message.

From Tom, my old account manager at Silverback. Breezy. Optimistic. Friendly. Asking how I am. Wondering where I've been. Wondering what my plans are. Having heard that I've left, been made redundant. Some money in my pocket, he hopes.

But if I'm in between things, he might have some freelance work. If I'm interested. Major new project. Big push. Quite glamorous too. Right up my street. Can't say too much. But I've worked with this client before and they loved my work. Just some copywriting. Big budget. Good rate. Give him a call if I'm interested. Oh yeah the name of the project: The Group. For Torrid Media.

So things fall apart, and they come full circle. There is a perfect symmetry at play that I find attractive. There is no beginning, there is no end.

And if I've not been able to make sense of the way things work, or the way people are, or even come to know myself through all of this, at least here there is a structure that I can understand. And a vicious irony, which is, oh so familiar.

I look at my room. My temporary home, where I have lived for so many years, and already there is so little trace of my ever being here.

I look at all my possessions, carefully sorted, stacked and packed. So little to show for what I am or to mark my passing. So little to leave behind after I am gone.

I feel a pang of anxiety. These are my things. And I don't know where they are going, or what I'm going to do with them. My future is so uncertain. My plans are so sketchy.

When I leave it'll be like I never was, and when I arrive at the place where I am going, there will be no welcome.

No one will know me. No one will care.

I pick up the phone and start to dial. It rings, once, twice, three times. And then I hear his voice.

'Hello, Silverback Communications, Tom speaking.'

'Hey Tom, how are you? It's Khaled.'

'Hey how are you? Good to hear from you,' I hear a genuine warmth that draws me in.

'Good, Tom, really good. Listen, mate. Just a quick call. I got your message. Listen, I'm really glad you called about that job, I mean thanks for thinking of me.'

'That's alright mate don't mention it, so do you fancy it?'

'Yeah you know that's why I calling.'

I look again at the things in my rooms. Everything almost forgotten already.

'Yeah Tom, that's why I'm calling, it does sound good and all but thanks you know errm, I just, I mean I can't do it. Thanks anyway, but I can't.'

I say goodbye quickly, and put down the phone, before I can talk myself round.

I look around my room, and I know it's not me. I look at my possessions; my things and I know that I can live without them all.

And I think again about how far I've come and what it would mean to go back to where I started. It'd be just the same as standing still, which could only ever be an unsatisfactory ending.

Light,
by Craig Taylor

ISBN 1 905315 00 7 • £6.99

"Before you know it you've read 100 pages in a sitting. Extremely compelling and delightfully unusual, it would make a wonderful bitter sweet film in the vein of Withnail and I."
Time Out

CRAIG TAYLOR

LIGHT

reverb

Light is a poignant story of love, loss and English summer. After the death of his father and the loss of his job, Ben's reacquaintance with a childhood friend pitches him into a glamorous life among a wealthy, rural set.

In a milieu of infidelity, corruption, cash and unrequited love, the narrator inadvertently achieves artistic fame. Through revelations of long-buried love, mix-ups and malice, an accident occurs and an innocent party takes the blame.

Inspired by the art and media world of the late 1990s, when an idealistic and transient glamour created millions for the elite of the new economy, Light has a strong claim to being the English *Great Gatsby*.

STEVE REDWOOD

WHO NEEDS CLEOPATRA?

reverb

Who Needs Cleopatra?
by Steve Redwood

ISBN 1 905315 03 1 • £7.99

"Where does a circle begin? When I met Bertie and we made our first journey through time? Or was the real beginning when I stumbled across that astonishing 16th-century notebook in an Italian farmhouse? But then long before that, in a way, I had provided a wife for Cain, and so allowed myself to exist in the first place..."

What made the Mona Lisa smile? How did Rasputin die? And what *really* happened at Roswell?

Despite the best attempts of the sardonic narrator 'N' and his hapless sidekick Bertie to solve historical mysteries, all they find is constant danger – and the sneaking suspicion that they have inadvertently created the very events they are supposed to be investigating.

This richly comic novel does for history what Jasper fforde did for literature - join Leonardo da Vinci, Boadicea, Cain (and Mabel) on a rollercoaster quest through time where the future (and the present) of humanity itself is at stake.

Grief, by Ed Lark

ISBN 1 905315 02 3 • £6.99

"The clouds were ugly and dark as scabs. I loved Keeku for a moment. A cab drove past me and I pretended it was a horse, swore it was a horse. I chased it down the street telling it to giddy-up. I hated Keeku now, the stupidity of her beautiful neck, the docile barges of her thighs and her mouth with the wet hole in it where the words came out."

Juan has left his past behind for the seductions of the city and the Crystal Realm – a world of ever-changing fashion, daily plastic surgery, mind-altering drugs and bizarre sex.

He effortlessly climbs the social hierarchy, gaining money and power until the city thrills to his every move – but something is missing from his life, which perhaps only the picaresque troupe of troubadours who are trekking across the desert in search of him can explain.

Grief is both a unique dystopia, or perhaps an interpretation of the present, and a remarkable psychological fantasy, disturbing, witty and moving by turns.

aboutreverb

reverb isn't a traditional publisher. We think of it as a cross between an online community of readers and an independent record label. Why a record label? Because we publish books that have broadly the same 'sound' - contemporary literary fiction with an edge. This edge can be humorous, it can be thought-provoking, but it is something that makes the book stand out from the crowd. We hope that if a reader has enjoyed one **reverb** book then they will enjoy the others.

reverbforwriters

Unless they are already successful, writers tend to get treated pretty badly. At **reverb** we are trying to do things a little differently:

- **Give new writers a chance -** we are committed to publishing 50 new writers over the next five years.
- **Fast but meaningful feedback -** most traditional publishers will leave unsolicited manuscripts on the slush pile for months; many are rejected unread. At **reverb** we promise to give an answer to any writer who follows our submission guidelines *within seven days*. If we do reject the material we will always try and give a constructive critique rather than simply a three-line rejection letter.
- **Working in partnership -** we view writers as talent to be nurtured rather than a commodity to be exploited. We pay high royalty rates and the lion's share of rights sales always goes to the writer.
- **Developing new talent -** we have dedicated a section of the **readreverb.com** site to information and support for new writers. We will also run free workshops in which our writers will share their experience and knowledge to help new authors develop their work.

aboutreverb

reverbforreaders

Without readers there would be no publishing, so we have
set up **reverb**review to create interest in all writers, not
just the ones that we publish. **reverb**review is a weekly
newsletter that contains book reviews, an in-depth look at
an iconic author or book and articles from readers on books
that have changed their lives. **readreverb.com** contains an
archive of **reverb**reviews, features and news stories from
the world of books.

reverbforretailers

Independent booksellers are the backbone of the trade, but
more often than not get treated like the poor cousin by
large publishing companies. At Reverb we are dedicated to
supporting the independent trade through offers, marketing
material and author visits.

---

reverbreview

At **reverb** we're passionate about hundreds of writers – not just
the ones that we publish - which is why we set up **reverb**review.

reverbreview is a regular email newsletter containing
book news, reviews and a feature article on the work of a
contemporary writer.

Because we are so passionate about the writers that we publish
we'll also be giving away ten signed copies of our books to
reverbreview readers every week, plus we'll offer you the chance
to attend special events to meet our writers and hear them
talk about their work.

For more information please visit **www.readreverb.com**

Printed in the United Kingdom
by Lightning Source UK Ltd.
104391UKS00001B/4-78